"Nice work," Dan commented.

"Thank you," she murmured.

"You need to ask my mother to teach you to needlepoint. You're a natural."

She chuckled and their eyes met and held. Her face warmed.

"So this is what your rescue team is all about," Beth said quietly to Dan.

"Not always such happy endings. We could use someone like you on the team," Dan murmured.

Beth met his gaze and paused. His smile caught her and she lost focus, lured for a brief reckless moment into considering a future outside of her carefully laid plans.

Dan Gallagher stirred something in her that she wasn't familiar with. For the very first time in her entire life, she was tempted to consider acting on her feelings instead of using her head.

She averted her gaze and rational thought once again took over.

Paradise was, after all, merely a stop on the road to her tomorrow. Dan Gallagher, a pleasant detour.

That was the reality she had to cling to.

Books by Tina Radcliffe

Love Inspired

The Rancher's Reunion
Oklahoma Reunion
Mending the Doctor's Heart
Stranded with the Rancher

TINA RADCLIFFE

has been dreaming and scribbling for years. Originally from Western, New York, she left home for a tour of duty with the Army Security Agency stationed in Augsburg, Germany, and ended up in Tulsa, Oklahoma. While living in Tulsa she spent ten years as a certified oncology RN. A former library cataloger, she now works for a large mail-order pharmacy. Tina currently resides in the foothills of Colorado, where she writes heartwarming romance. You can reach her at www.tinaradcliffe.com.

Stranded with the Rancher

Tina Radcliffe

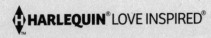

HARLEQUIN® LOVE INSPIRED®

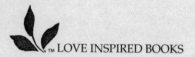

LOVE INSPIRED BOOKS

Recycling programs
for this product may
not exist in your area.

ISBN-13: 978-0-373-81790-0

STRANDED WITH THE RANCHER

Copyright © 2014 by Tina M. Radcliffe

www.Harlequin.com

Printed in U.S.A.

Brethren, I do not count myself to have apprehended; but one thing I do, forgetting those things which are behind and reaching forward to those things which are ahead, I press toward the goal for the prize of the upward call of God in Christ Jesus.

—*Philippians* 3:13–14

While it's true that it always takes a village, this book took several villages.

I am indebted to rancher Ivan Connealy and his wife, Western inspirational author (romantic comedy with cowboys) Mary Connealy for answering my endless questions on cows and ranches and farming. I don't know how you do it.

Thank you to Karen Robinson, CPM, RM, President of the Colorado Midwives Association (www.coloradomidwives.org) for her generosity with answers and quick response to my questions.

Many thanks to Rich from Vickery Motorsports in Denver, Colorado, for taking time from his workday to talk to me on the phone about snowmobiles.

Thank you, Vince Mooney, for beta-reading my proposal with a reader's eagle eye for detail.

My emergency medical expert was Tom Radcliffe, former EMT who works for Rural Metro Ambulance and also is my best reader.

All errors are wholly mine.

Thank you to my agent, Meredith Bernstein, the woman in my corner who believes in me.

There's a special place in heaven for deadline buddies. A shout-out to R.B., M.V.M and M.T. Thank you for your support.

Finally, thank you to assistant editor Giselle Regus, who helped me find the jewels in my prose and brought this book to delivery.

Chapter One

"Small towns always look best from my rearview mirror," Elizabeth Rogers said. She tugged on her coat and turned to look at her cousin.

"Beth, you aren't even giving Paradise a chance," Ben Rogers returned.

"Sure I am. I had lunch and a tour of the hospital and clinic with the medical director. Did I mention how much I like your new clinic?" Beth paused. "But I'm not really interested in the position."

"Uh-huh. I'm thinking you can't see anything but New York City."

"I won't deny that I'm excited about New York." Beth reached out to touch Ben's arm. "But you know I'm glad you found happiness with Sara here in Paradise, right?" She smiled. "This place is perfect for you—just not for me. I guess I'm a city girl at heart."

"Not always. Remember when we lived in that little town near the Four Corners?"

"That wasn't a town. It was a gas station and half a grocery story. It reminded me of the truck stop where my mother dumped me."

Ben winced. "Ah, Beth. I'm sorry." He ran a hand through his hair. "I didn't mean to bring up bad memories."

She raised a palm. "No worries. I was very grateful that your parents took me in, but I've never quite forgiven them for moving us there."

"Rural medicine. You know that's their life."

"Is it okay to admit I'm relieved those days are over?"

"Not for me," he said. "God and Paradise changed that."

"You made a choice, Ben. And I'm trying to do the same. I don't want to ever be in a position where I have to choose between two evils again."

Ben shook his head.

He didn't get it. Beth sighed. *No one did. Time to change the subject.*

"I really love this house." She shoved her mittens and wool scarf into her soft leather, oversize tote and then looked around the guest room of the quaint Craftsman bungalow.

"Thank you," he replied.

"Too bad it's not somewhere else."

Ben chuckled. "Do you have everything?" he asked.

Beth walked around the large four-poster bed.

"Aha! Cell phone charger. I would have been very unhappy if I'd left this behind." After unplugging the cord, she straightened, her gaze moving to the window. "It's really snowing now. We'd better go."

"Your flight isn't until two." He glanced at his watch. "The airport is less than forty-five minutes away. That puts you there more than three hours early."

"And that's fine with me."

"Okay. Okay. Let's tell Sara we're leaving. I think she's with the babies."

He picked up Beth's suitcase and she followed him down the stairwell to the first floor. His wife, Sara, stood in the living room between two baby swings. She was talking to a tall man in a black ski jacket with a black Stetson on his head, while simultaneously rocking identical babies in their swings.

"Dan. What are you doing here?" Ben called.

"Hey, Doc." The cowboy grinned, his glance moving to Beth.

"Dan Gallagher, this is my cousin, Dr. Elizabeth Rogers."

The cowboy removed his hat and nodded politely before putting the hat back on. "Nice to meet you, ma'am."

Beth shot him a distracted smile, her gaze pulled to the window, where enormous snowflakes obliterated the view. She needed to leave. *Now.*

Sara turned to Ben. "Dan brought the twins'

antibiotics. The pharmacy is closing early due to the forecast."

"Much appreciated," Ben said. "This is their second ear infection in six months and none of us are happy about it."

As they chatted, Beth chewed her lip. She wasn't going to panic. *Relax. Just relax.* She repeated the mantra.

"Maybe we'd better get going, Ben," she suggested in her calmest voice.

"Ma'am, I don't think you're going anywhere for a while."

Beth inhaled and avoided looking at Dan Gallagher, as though she could erase what he'd just said by ignoring it. "I have to go," she finally stated.

"Weather report has recently upgraded the storm. Conditions are ripe for this to be the worst one of the season. The roads are closing as fast as that snow is moving in."

"But it's the end of March," Beth quickly countered. "It'll be April in a couple of days."

"Welcome to Colorado," Dan said.

"Ben?" she pleaded.

"Beth, I know. I get it. But I can't control Mother Nature. If this storm is coming in as fast as Dan says it is, then there won't be any airplanes going anywhere."

"I've *got* to be in New York by Monday." She tamped down a bubble of panic, searching for a rational thought. "Surely things will clear up by morning?"

"That could happen," Sara commented. She reached out to pat Beth's arm. "Sometimes our mountain storms hit quickly and then leave."

Dan gave a shake of his head, indicating he doubted that was going to be the case today. "I'm making a delivery in Gunbarrel," he said. "I'd be happy to take you that far. You can reevaluate the situation tomorrow. They've got a small hotel with an airport shuttle. At least you'd be halfway to the airport."

Beth brightened at the suggestion. "Yes, that would be great. Thank you."

"I thought you were on call tonight," Ben said, looking at Dan.

"On call?" Beth asked.

"Dan's a key member of our Paradise Clinic Snowmobile Rescue Team," Ben said.

Dan shrugged at the words. "I traded shifts. My brother is out of town for a prosthesis fitting and left me in charge of the ranch."

"What are you doing in town then?" Ben asked.

"With this weather we were short staffed at the pharmacy as well, so I came in for a bit."

"You left the cows alone?" Ben said the words with a laugh.

"Oh, you know. The whole family pitches in. My mother can handle things in a pinch."

He nodded. "How *is* Joe doing?"

"One step forward and two steps back."

"We're praying," Sara said.

"Thanks." Dan's gaze met Beth's. "Well, we'd better get moving."

She turned and hugged first Ben and then Sara. "Thank you for a lovely visit." Beth patted baby Carolyn and her twin, Amanda, on their soft heads and smiled wistfully at them. A pang of longing filled her as she allowed herself to imagine what it would be like to be married and happy like her cousin. To have a child.

"They are so beautiful," she murmured.

"Give them five minutes. They both just ate and forgot they have ear infections in progress. You won't want to be here tonight when they remember again," Sara said.

"I'll be back. As soon as my schedule permits," Beth said.

Dan Gallagher's hand covered hers as they reached for the suitcase at the same time.

She froze, embarrassed.

"I've got it," he said. Following her, he carried the bag into the small anteroom and then closed the door behind them before staring out the front door at the blizzard, which had risen out of nowhere in less than an hour's time.

A big silver pickup truck was parked in front of the house. The tarp that covered a snowmobile in the flatbed strained against its ties, while the edges of the blue fabric flapped furiously.

"That's quite a wind," Beth said. She wrapped her wool scarf around her neck.

Dan nodded as he pulled on a pair of dark leather gloves and picked up her suitcase again. "Ready?" he asked.

"Yes."

When he opened the door a gust of wind rushed past and slammed into her, bringing stinging flakes along as well.

Heads down, they dashed through the nearly ankle-deep snow to the curb. Yanking open the passenger door, Dan carefully helped her up and into the vehicle. Chivalry was still alive in Paradise, Beth mused.

He adjusted his Stetson against the snow before he slid the suitcase into the backseat and then came around the truck to the driver's side and got in. The man was well over six feet tall and the space inside the cab seemed to noticeably shrink as he settled in his seat. For the first time Beth really looked at him.

Beneath the brim of the Stetson his black hair was trimmed short, and the shadow of a beard accented his square jaw. When he turned slightly and his gaze met hers, Beth found herself staring into calm, slate-colored eyes. She turned away, embarrassed to be caught.

She cleared her throat. "I, ah, I really appreciate

this." She brushed the snow off her hair and reached for her seat belt.

"Not a problem." He pulled on his own seat belt.

"What would you be doing if I wasn't tagging along?"

"I was heading home. This is just another day for me. Winter in Paradise means that some days getting home requires a bit more patience than other days."

"Where is it you live?" she asked.

"Outside of Paradise."

"And where is Gunbarrel?"

"A little bit farther down the road," Dan said.

"You're sure we can get there?"

"Ma'am, I'm only sure of a few things in life. But I can tell you this—if I can't get through then no one can."

The CB radio crackled as the truck roared like a wakening lion. A moment later the massive windshield wipers began to slowly shovel the snow away in large wedges. The big blades moved with a thumping rhythm.

You won't make it. You won't make it. They chanted the words over and over again.

Biting her lower lip, Beth ignored the mocking and focused on trying to see the road ahead. She had to make it to New York. She'd spent too many years working her way out of her circumstances to once again be at the mercy of something she couldn't control.

"What's in New York?" Dan finally asked. They'd driven in companionable silence for several miles, and though the driving was slow, they were well past the outskirts of town.

"I have a locum tenens position that starts on Monday," Beth answered.

"Locum tenens? You're a temp doctor?" He couldn't help the surprise in his voice.

"Yes."

Dan cocked his head and shot her a glance. "If you don't mind my asking, why would you want to be a temp doc instead of having your own practice?"

"I like traveling. New cities. New adventures."

"Ah, you're one of those." His gaze again left the road for a moment and met her cool blue eyes.

"Excuse me?" Annoyance laced her voice as she pushed strands of toffee-brown hair away from her face and stared at him.

"I just mean you're a wanderer."

"A wanderer?" She paused briefly, considering his words. "You're implying I'm lost?"

Dan held back a chuckle, recalling the Tolkien quote, "Not all who wander are lost." Another glance at Dr. Elizabeth Rogers told him she wouldn't be amused by the reference.

"No, ma'am," he finally returned.

As if reading his mind, she exhaled sharply, obviously more than a little defensive. "You know, there's nothing wrong with—"

Her voice trailed off when the vehicle suddenly lurched forward.

From habit Dan reached out an arm to protect his passenger.

When the truck jerked to the left he gripped the steering wheel tightly with both hands, struggling to maintain control.

Something didn't feel right with the steering. Too much play. He'd noticed the same thing earlier in the week, but had dismissed it as his imagination. Now he chastised himself for not taking the truck in to be checked.

"You okay?" he asked as the vehicle slowed.

She nodded. "That was scary."

"Yeah. Sorry, patch of ice."

"The temperatures are dropping already?"

"There's a sheet of ice on the roads from that snow-rain mix that was coming down first," Dan said.

"Maybe this wasn't such a good idea. I've put you at risk."

"Naw. I told you I'd be out on the roads anyway, to get home." Dan turned up the defroster, hoping to clear the clouded window. "But it might be a good idea to call ahead to the Gunbarrel Hotel and let them know you're coming."

Beth pulled off her gloves and dug a cell phone out of her tote. "No reception."

"Once we get to the other side of that hill you should get something."

"What hill?" She narrowed her eyes as she peered through the windshield. "All I can see are pine trees and those tall poles."

"Snow poles. But trust me, we're almost past the hill. I've pretty much got this road memorized. I spend a lot of time back and forth, making deliveries."

"Deliveries?" Beth asked as she put the phone away.

"I'm a pharmacist."

"A pharmacist who makes deliveries?"

"Why not?" Dan smiled, amused at her reaction. "Fact is, sometimes it's the only way I can get things to my patients."

She glanced out the back window toward the flatbed. "And you're on a snowmobile rescue team?"

He nodded. "Yeah. So I know this area inside and out."

"What do you do as a volunteer?"

"Whatever Dr. Rogers tells me to do." He grinned.

"Ben is your boss?"

"Dr. Sara *and* Dr. Ben are. Ben manages the unit and Sara is his backup. There are six of us and each member has their own area of expertise. I'm an AIFLP."

Beth stared blankly at him.

"Advanced interfacility life support paramedic."

"You're a critical care paramedic?" she asked.

"The state of Colorado doesn't have critical care paramedics…*yet*. Approval is tied up in government red tape."

"I'm still impressed. That's quite a specialty out in the field."

Dan shrugged. "I guess so, but I'm basically in it for the perks."

"Perks?"

"Occasionally they let me ride in the helicopter."

A smile parted her lips and her blue eyes sparkled, transforming her reserved expression. Dan was caught off guard when dimples appeared. Apparently Dr. Rogers's good humor had been restored.

He made a mental note not to annoy her again. They were in for a long day and he didn't need to be at odds with his passenger in the confining space of the truck cab. Besides, he liked it when she smiled. Elizabeth Rogers was easy on the eyes.

"Have we passed your place?" she asked.

"No, at the snail's pace we're going, it'll be a bit. I'm off the beaten path to the east. Small ranch at the base of the mountains."

"You're a rancher, as well?" she asked.

"Not me. My brother. He runs about two hundred head of cattle."

They rounded a bend in the road and Dan nodded toward the phone in her lap. "Why don't you check for signal strength again?"

Beth picked up her phone. "Yes. Got it."

"Great. Use my phone." He pulled a cell from his jacket pocket. "I have the sheriff's office on speed dial. Dispatch can connect you to the Gunbarrel Hotel."

She shook her head. "It's a recording."

"What's it say?"

"Call 9-1-1 if it's an emergency. Due to a heavy volume of calls, unable to…" Beth released a breath. "What now?"

"When is your flight?" he asked.

"It's not until two, but it's the last Alamosa-to-Denver flight until Monday. Then I still have to connect to New York." Turning to the window, she hid her expression.

"You think they're going to hold a blizzard against you?"

"I think it's likely I won't get the position. They need a physician now, not later."

"If you don't mind my asking, what's so important about a temp position?"

She looked at him. "This particular medical group auditions all candidates for their practice by allowing them to work as a locum tenens first. It's the only way you get in."

"I take it the competition is stiff."

"There were over one hundred applicants. In the end, only two of us were chosen. If either of us is a good match for their team we'll be offered a permanent job."

"What's the catch?"

"The catch?"

"You could get a job anywhere. Why this practice? What makes it so special?"

"It's been my dream for as long as I can remember."

"What? Big city and big bucks?" The words spilled out before he could consider how bitter he sounded for a man who thought he was long over his past.

When her eyes flashed, he knew he'd irritated her again. *So much for his good intentions.*

Before he could correct his misstep the truck began to vibrate with the fierce stuttering of the antilock brake system kicking in. Dan grabbed the wheel firmly. "Hold on. We're sliding."

The big truck continued to skid right, until it suddenly fishtailed and changed direction.

They were both jolted sideways as metal scraped against metal, the sound raw and screeching as the vehicle crashed through a guardrail and headed straight for an enormous conifer.

"Lord," he said beneath his breath. "We could use a little help."

Bracing himself, Dan again instinctively shot an

arm out to protect his passenger from hitting the dash. He effectively held her shoulders back against the leather seat.

Time was suspended as the truck was shoved against the tree, which struck the left front tire and bumper before settling against the driver's side door.

The pickup shifted and finally was still.

The only sounds were the swish of the wipers and their ragged breathing.

"Are you okay?" Dan finally asked.

"Yes. Are you?"

"Yeah." He released a low whistle. "That was close."

"Why didn't the air bags deploy?" she asked.

"Not a frontal impact. The side impact wasn't enough to deploy them."

She nodded and looked around. "What are we going to do?"

"First, I'm going to assess the damage and then we'll figure out exactly where we are."

"Do you want help?"

"No, thanks. Best if you stay in the truck." Dan shouldered the door, which resisted. Shoving all his weight against it, he was finally able to wedge it open enough to squeeze his way out and through the branches of the tree the truck had nestled against.

Beth grabbed her phone from the floor and checked the GPS app. No signal. She tried the compass application before it occurred to her she couldn't read a compass, anyhow.

Was she completely useless outside of a medical clinic? Why hadn't she become a Girl Scout? A little voice answered, *Because you never lived in one place long enough.*

A knock at her window made her jump.

Dan.

Beth opened her door.

He shook the snow off his hat and coat before he ducked his head inside the truck. Only inches away, she breathed in the scent of pine and man as he moved even closer, out of the wind. Tiny crystals of snow clung to his lashes, and Beth stared, mesmerized.

"Compass?" he asked, with a glance at her phone.

"Yes. But I can't figure it out."

"That's okay. I've got a better idea."

She raised her brows in question.

"The truck's not going anywhere. Rim and tire are a mess. No telling what else got damaged in the crash. It's snowing too hard to find the mile markers, so I'm going to take the snowmobile out and verify our location."

"You're leaving me?" Beth clutched his sleeve. Suddenly the job in New York seemed the least of her concerns.

"I'll be back."

"No," she whispered adamantly. "Take me with

you." She'd been reduced to pleading like a child. But she didn't care. He wasn't going to leave her.

"Elizabeth." Dan's voice was steady, firm and reassuring, talking her down from the ledge of fear she had climbed. "I'll be right back."

"Beth. I'm just Beth." The words were hollow. She stared at the snow accumulating on the windshield. Flake upon flake piled up, like a smothering blanket, until she could barely see daylight through the glass.

"Beth."

Turning, she met his gaze. Dan Gallagher had kind eyes.

"We're going to be fine." His lips curved into a gentle smile. "Okay?"

"Okay." A single word to rest her future on.

"Here are the truck keys. If you absolutely have to, start the engine and run the heater. Keep the emergency brake on."

"You said you're coming right back."

"That's right." He nodded, but continued talking. "I've got a first aid kit and crash cart supplies in the backseat in those two tackle boxes. The portable defibrillator is under the seat. There's also emergency food and water in that red box. If you have to get out of the vehicle, stay away from the trees. We're way too close to the ravine."

"We could have gone into the ravine?"

"Those trees stopped us."

Stunned, she was silent for a moment. "I'd prefer not to die today if you don't mind."

"I'll try to remember that." He stared deeply into her eyes as if searching for something. "Do you pray?" Dan asked.

"What?"

"Do you pray?"

"I used to," Beth murmured.

"Now would be a good time to start again." He tossed his Stetson in the backseat, turned up his collar and gently shut the door.

The truck jostled as he lowered the liftgate and slid the snowmobile off the flatbed. The engine roared to life and a moment later the snowmobile's headlight illuminated the truck and moved past. Barely a second later he was gone; swallowed up by the swirling snow.

Beth closed her eyes and did what she always did when she was afraid. She began to count backward from one hundred, taking calming breaths.

He'll be back.

Still the suffocating terror pressed in. *That's what your mother said. And she never came back.*

"Eighty-eight. Eighty-seven."

It had been a very long time since she had prayed. She'd spent her entire adult life focused on her goals, so she would never be in that place of desperation again. That vulnerable point, where God was her only hope.

Yet here she was in the middle of nowhere. Lost. Her shot at the job she'd been waiting her entire career for was slipping through her fingers, and a cowboy pharmacist was out there risking his life on her behalf.

"Sixty-four."

How had everything spun out of her careful control?

Beth glanced around the truck cab. Exhaling, she watched a puff of breath appear like a small cloud, then evaporate.

Pray, Dan had said.

Did God even remember her?

Lord, this is Bethy Rogers. I really need Your help.

Chapter Two

Beth exhaled. Her panicked breaths were accomplishing nothing more than creating a veil of condensation on the windshield. She wiped at the moisture with a gloved hand and then unbuttoned her wool coat. Then she checked her phone yet again.

Dan had been gone thirty minutes.

Her mind continued to race back and forth between worst-case scenarios.

When the CB gave a static squawk Beth glanced down at the black box mounted between the passenger and driver seats. Maybe she should try to call someone on the radio to send help. Who would she contact? Ben? No, she didn't want Ben or Sara out here risking their lives.

Yet Dan Gallagher was. For her. Did he have family waiting for him?

Beth swallowed hard, considering the implications of her dogged decision to get to Gunbarrel.

Calm down.

Dan's job is dealing with snow emergencies. He'll be fine. He'll be back soon.

Right?

She leaned against the seat and stared at the ceiling of the cab. "Please, Lord, keep Dan safe."

Twice in one day she'd called upon the Lord. The realization stunned her. It had no doubt stunned Him, as well.

Moments later the distant rumble of a snowmobile engine broke the silence.

Apparently He was still listening.

She whispered a thank-you and shoved open the door of the truck.

The moment her booted foot pushed through the deep snow and made contact with the ground, she realized her error. Six inches of March snow covered a slick surface.

Her feet scissored back and forth in a crazed dance as she made a frantic attempt to gain traction on the slippery ground.

"Oomph."

Beth landed unceremoniously on her left side. Who knew snow could hurt so much? She rolled to her back and lay there, regrouping, as the snowflakes continued to fall on her.

The hint of gas fumes tickled her nose a moment before Dan appeared. She barely knew the man, but as he towered above her, dressed all in black, with the helmet on and his goggles around his neck, she dared to release a small smile.

Oh, he looked good. Very good.

"You okay?" he asked.

Beth met his concerned gaze. "I'll be fine," she murmured, as she struggled to a sitting position and then wiped the snow from her face.

"How do you know?"

"Because I'm a doctor and doctors don't lie." She arched a brow. "Hippocratic oath."

Dan chuckled, a wry smile curling his full lips before he suddenly sobered. "Loose translation. Besides, I wasn't doubting your integrity. I was assessing you. No pain in the arm or shoulder? You landed awfully hard on that left side."

"You saw me fall?"

"Yeah. Sorry."

She sighed and blew strands of hair out of her eyes. Her last attempt at dignity disappeared like the vaporous clouds she exhaled each time she spoke.

"Let me help you up."

"No, I can—"

Before she could continue her protest, he crouched down, wrapped an arm around her waist and heaved her to a standing position, all in one swift and heroic movement.

"You sure you're okay?" he asked again.

Beth gave a tight little nod and then scooted inches away from him until her backside was flat against the passenger seat of the open cab. He was close, much too close. Close enough that the heat from the tall cowboy reached out to warm her.

The fall she could handle. The genuine concern in Dan's eyes, combined with the unexpected comfort and strength of his arm… Well, that was another matter. She brushed ineffectually at her limp, wet jeans.

Oblivious to the fact that he was right in the middle of her personal space, Dan leaned against the inside of the door, his broad shoulders shielding her from the weather.

"Do you want the good news first or the bad news?"

"Bad new first. Always."

"We're not going to make it to Gunbarrel tonight."

"Okay," she said.

"Really? You're okay with that?" Confused, he rubbed a hand over his face.

"Let's just say my priorities have shifted considerably."

He shook his head as if he understood. "Okay, then, well, the good news is we're about ten miles outside of Paradise. Closer to the ranch than anywhere else."

"The ranch." She nodded. "And your wife, she won't mind that you're bringing home a strange woman?"

"Are you strange?"

Beth fought the urge to laugh.

"I'm not married." He stared at a spot above her head. "Well, not anymore," he murmured. "We're going to head to my mother's. She has a big, old house with lots of room. Now that the family is grown, it's only her, and my daughter, who stays with her after school."

"You have a daughter?"

Dan's face lit up. "Yeah. She's six."

"You're sure that your mother won't mind the intrusion?"

"Oh, you know how mothers are."

"Not really."

Dan narrowed his eyes at her comment. "I can tell you that my mother likes nothing more than feeding people and clucking over them. She's out of practice, with an empty house."

"If you say so. What about your cows? I thought you had cows to take care of."

"The cows are at the ranch."

Beth blinked, confused.

"My mother lives in the main house at the ranch. My brother and I have our own cabins nearby."

"Your *entire family* lives in the same place?"

"Yeah." He paused, obviously taken aback. "But you make it sound like we should be on a reality TV show or something."

Beth bit her lip and barely resisted a laugh. "No,

I'm sorry. It's me who's behaving oddly. Not you. I'm not accustomed to all this familial closeness."

"I take it you don't live near your family?"

"Ben and his parents are my only relatives. Plus Sara and the girls now, too, I guess." *And that was enough sharing.* She glanced at the backseat. "May I bring my suitcase?"

"I'll come back for your bag."

"I need my clothes."

"Could you shove a few things in your tote bag? I've got to take the portable defibrillator with us. Too expensive a toy to leave out here. The snowmobile doesn't have much storage space, and the defibrillator will take up a lot of it."

"Sure. Okay, I can do that."

Dan opened the backseat and Beth leaned in to unzip the side of her suitcase.

"Do you mind turning your head?" she asked.

"Turn my head?" He narrowed his eyes.

"This is rather embarrassing. I have, um, personal items."

"And I have two sisters."

"That's nice, but I'm an only child. *So turn your head, please.*"

"Yes, ma'am."

He laughed and the sound—rich, deep and warm—caught her off guard.

Beth smiled as she grabbed her flannel pajamas and a change of clothes. With a quick peek to be sure he really wasn't looking, she shoved in a few more things.

"Ready?"

"Yes."

"We should hurry. The storm is getting worse."

"How can you tell?"

Dan looked up at the dark gray sky. "See how the wind is kicking up again?"

She tilted her head back. The clouds were moving quickly and the aspens had begun to wave, whipping snow that looked like white dust into the air.

"We won't be able to go anywhere in whiteout conditions."

He was besting her worst-case scenario list without even trying.

"And I'm guessing pitching a tent in the middle of a blizzard isn't on your list of fun and adventurous things to do," Dan added.

"You're not serious."

"Oh, yeah. I am. The snowmobile has an emergency survival kit in the extra storage bin." Dan moved closer and Beth stepped back, nearly slipping again.

"Whoa." He grabbed her by the shoulders, keeping her upright.

"Oh!" A cry of pain ripped from her lips.

"You *did* hurt yourself." His words were a warm whisper against her hair.

"I'm fine. Possibly a sprain, if anything."

"We'll check it out at the ranch."

Beth frowned. *Not likely.*

"Okay. Bundle up. It'll be cold. And wrap that scarf so it covers your mouth."

Ben lifted the backseat of the snowmobile and pulled out another pair of goggles from a storage space before he put the small portable defibrillator and her tote bag inside the compartment.

He breathed onto the goggle lenses before handing them to her.

"I want you to pay close attention to how I move on the machine. If I lean forward, you lean forward. If I stand, you stand."

Beth nodded.

"Just follow my lead. It's a lot like a motorcycle for the passenger," he said with a shrug.

"I've never ridden a motorcycle," Beth admitted as she adjusted the goggles.

Dan raised a brow, but didn't utter a word of surprise, and was kind enough not to mention her previous claims of seeking adventure.

"One last thing," he said. "If there are any problems and it looks like I'm going to have to roll the machine and then jump off, I want you to jump away and uphill, as far from the snowmobile as you can."

Beth gulped. Her gaze met his.

"Stay alert and keep your hands on me at all times. Understand?"

Again she gave a nod of understanding, this time accompanied by a smile of false bravado.

Reaching into the flatbed, he pulled out a black helmet identical to his.

When he handed it to her, Beth slipped it on her head.

Dan yanked off his gloves. "I'm going to adjust the strap. Don't be in a rush to step away from me again or you might fall."

Beth stood still, her cheeks tingling with embarrassment as she stared straight ahead at the dark stubble on his jaw and the patch of skin visible where his jacket met his neck. She feigned composure as his warm fingers brushed against her chin.

Finally, she dared to meet his eyes.

They reflected only compassion. "It really is going to be all right," he said softly.

The man was intuitive.

As a physician, Beth was accustomed to being the one doing the reassuring, but somehow things had gotten turned around. Dan had told her everything was going to be all right, and she believed him. Believed him, though she'd missed her flight, her shoulder was probably sprained and she was headed to a destination unknown. Yet an unlikely peace had settled over her. How could that be?

Possibly the altitude.

"Okay," Dan said as he pulled his gloves back on. "I'm going to get on first." He inclined his head toward the snowmobile before smoothly sliding onto the machine.

On her second awkward attempt, Beth finally landed in the seat. She sat stiffly behind him.

"Put your arms around me," he called over his shoulder. "And don't let go."

Don't let go. Beth loosely wrapped her arms around his waist. Her helmet was inches from his back.

The engine revved and then the machine moved forward, propelling her backward with force.

Beth tightened her hold on Dan, gripping his jacket fiercely. She tucked her face behind his broad back, hiding from the stinging moisture of the rapidly falling snow.

Hypervigilant, Beth monitored the nuances of the engine and the man, adjusting herself to his movements. When he stood slightly and leaned forward as the snowmobile moved up an incline in the road, she did the same. They moved over the terrain, occasionally bouncing. Tension kept her rigid and silently praying that the machine wouldn't capsize, and that the weather wouldn't become severe enough to force them to stop.

Overhead, heavy gray clouds loomed ominously, while the wind chased them over an endless white vista.

As the minutes passed, Beth dared to relax, leaning back a tad to take in the snowy blur of the Colorado landscape. The air was crisp with the scent of pine and fresh snow. A small buzz of exhilaration thrummed through her as the wind rushed past, whipping her long hair into a frenzy.

Dan was right. Beth had lived all over, but "all over" looked like the same medical clinic and temporary housing in an endless stream of different cities.

Today's adventure had made one thing clear. She hadn't really experienced life at all.

Finally, the engine slowed and Dan signaled a left turn with his arm. Beth peeked around his shoulder, scanning the snowy horizon. The tension eased from her grip when she saw the hazy glow of lights ahead. Like a muted lighthouse beacon, they beckoned winter travelers up a long conifer-lined drive. Wherever they were, they had obviously arrived.

As they pulled up in front of a charming, two-story brick-and-clapboard house, Dan turned off the engine.

"We're home," he called over his shoulder.

Home? Beth released a nervous breath, along with a tiny smile of anticipation.

Thank You, Lord, for leading us home again to Gallagher Ranch.

Dan stared at the house for a moment, allowing the tension of the white-knuckle drive through the storm to slip from his body. The hundred-year-old farmhouse had weathered every storm the Sangre de Cristo Mountains had tossed its way. This particular system would be no exception. He came from a long line of Colorado pioneers and they had bred the same can-do spirit into him.

They knew how to handle winter in the mountains. There were backup generators, wood for the fireplace and enough canned goods to see them through six storms. Yeah, it was good to be home.

He got off the snowmobile and offered Beth a hand, easing her off the backseat.

Though her grip on his waist had been viselike, it was definitely not unpleasant to have her riding tandem. He'd expected the city girl would be a diva, but so far, well, she'd definitely proved him wrong.

Raising his arms overhead, Dan stretched his spine and then rotated his neck. "I'm going to open the garage," he said. "Be right back."

The echoing crunch of his boots as he crossed the yard filled the silence. Snow continued to fall like crystals into the night, but the pink glow of the mercury lights on the oversize storage building that served as a garage guided his way. He pulled open the big double doors, and they creaked in response. Inside, his mother's mini pickup was parked next to his brother's beat-up utility truck and the ranch ATV. Joe's personal truck was in the corner, covered with a tarp, waiting for his return.

Dan maneuvered the snowmobile in, then grabbed

Beth's tote and the defibrillator. He plugged in the defibrillator to charge the machine before closing the garage door. Walking to Beth, he nodded toward the house.

The front walkway and the wooden porch steps had recently been shoveled and sprinkled with snow melt, though the precipitation was quickly re-accumulating. On the porch a battered red shovel stood neatly next to the door, along with his daughter's small pink plastic shovel. Such an insignificant thing, but little Amy's imprint on his life never failed to make Dan smile.

He turned to Beth, and placed a finger to his lips before slowly opening the screen, then the front door. The loud, discordant plunking and banging of a piano greeted them.

Dan pulled off his helmet and goggles. Beth did the same.

She whispered to him, "May I use your restroom? I need to change into dry pants."

He pointed straight ahead. "First door on your left."

"Why are we whispering?" she asked.

"I don't want Millie to know we're home."

"Your daughter?"

"No, my dog."

Her eyes rounded. "Oh."

Beth slipped off her boots and put her helmet and goggles on the bright multicolored rag rug in front of the door. Taking her tote bag from Dan, she tip-toed down the hall.

He set his helmet next to hers and shut the door. The piano had stopped and the click of the door closing sounded in the room.

As if it had been a starting line gunshot, he prepared for the chaos to ensue. Barking erupted as Millie rushed from the back of the house to the front hall like a locomotive. Dan heard her well before he saw her. The lean black lab raced into the room, her nails clicking on the hardwood floor a minute before she leaped into the air and accosted him. Dan staggered back as the dog alternated between enthusiastic slobbering and mad barking.

"Down, Millie." He rubbed the good-natured animal's head and backside briskly. "Yeah, I missed you, too, girl."

Millie released a loud whine in dogspeak as she moved her paws to the floor and pranced in joyous circles at her master's return.

"Daddy, can we build a snowman?"

His six-year-old daughter waved a ruler through the air. Her round, gray eyes were serious as she peered up at him through oversize, red-framed plastic glasses minus the lenses. She'd been giving imaginary piano lessons to her dolls again.

"Not today, Pumpkin." Dan tweaked an inky black braid and gently tossed it over her shoulder. "You'd get buried in this storm."

"Tomorrow?"

"We'll see."

Amy didn't miss a beat, launching into her next request. "Can I watch TV?"

"May I." Elsie Gallagher bustled into the front entry, a basket of laundry in her arms. Her short black curls were peppered with gray and she wore her usual jeans and the sweatshirt du jour. Today's boasted a large bumblebee and the words Bee Cool. His mother the trendsetter.

"May I?" Amy repeated. "I already did my spelling."

"Joe called. He's stuck in Denver," Elsie continued. "He wants to be sure you're keeping a close eye on those cows. Says they might calve early."

"Big brother Joe thinks I'm a rookie. I already moved the cattle this morning. I'll check on them again after I eat. Mom, I should tell you I—"

His explanation was cut off by the sound of a door closing. All heads turned to look behind them as Elizabeth Rogers walked down the hall.

Beth had fixed her helmet hair, and her caramel-colored tresses tumbled around her shoulders from a side part, framing her heart-shaped face. Her skin glowed from the outdoors. Objectively speaking, the woman was a complete knockout.

His mother's jaw slackened, before she grinned as though she was privy to a huge secret.

And then Millie charged. "Whoa, whoa, Millie.

No." Dan barely managed to latch his hands onto the lab's collar and hold her back. "Sit."

Beth froze, blue eyes wide as Millie wriggled in a hearty attempt to properly greet their guest.

"Who *are you?*" Amy asked, her voice hushed and wondrous, as if she'd just stumbled upon a princess.

Dan couldn't resist a smile. He'd have to agree with his daughter. Beth Rogers did look like a princess. She was the prettiest thing to walk in their front door in a very long time.

Confusion crossed Beth's face as her gaze met his. "I'm Beth."

"Why, Daniel Davis Gallagher, you brought home a guest." His mother's words registered her stunned surprise. She set the laundry basket on the floor and straightened her sweatshirt.

"I've brought guests home before," Dan returned.

"Have you?" his mother replied.

"Do dogs count?" he asked.

Elsie laughed.

"Mom, this is Dr. Elizabeth Rogers. Beth, this is my mother, Elsie Gallagher, and *this*...is Pumpkin."

"Daddy!"

"I mean Amy." He grinned at his daughter.

"Rogers?" Elsie said. "Like Dr. Ben and Dr. Sara?"

Beth nodded. "Ben is my cousin."

"You're pretty," Amy gushed. She pulled down

her faux glasses for a better inspection as she inched toward Beth ever so slowly.

"Thank you," Beth said. "I like your glasses."

Amy smiled and tucked her face shyly into her shoulder.

Dan observed the interaction with interest.

"So how did you two meet?" his mother asked, her gaze moving from Dan to Beth, a knowing grin on her face.

He blinked and stepped back.

Oh, no.

No.

Surely his mother wasn't going to go down that road. "Docs Rogers's house. I offered to take Beth to Gunbarrel, but the storm derailed us." He looked at his mom. "When did you say Joe was getting back?"

His mother chuckled, reading his mind as usual. "You're out of luck, Danny boy."

Maybe bringing Beth to the house wasn't such a good idea, after all. His mother was a matchmaker. And she was good. Really good. She'd orchestrated his sisters' romances straight to the altar.

Dan held his own when Joe was around. Joe was the oldest and he protected his little brother. He shook his head. The odds were distinctly not in his favor.

Beth stood in the hallway, biting her lip in concentration as she attempted to sort out the dynamics. *Good luck with that.* He chuckled. The Gallagher house was always a little eccentric and the hormone-charged atmosphere changed as quickly as the Colorado weather.

He observed Beth for a moment. Any other lifetime and he'd be tripping over himself to get to know someone like her. Smart, beautiful and brave. Obviously not without some issues of her own, but seemingly capable of handling them with humor and grace. Yet, for today at least, the bottom line remained the same. Elizabeth Rogers was a woman passing through Paradise. A city girl to boot.

Like Amy's momma.

He and his mother were going to have to have a little chat, because he sure wasn't going to step into the same cow patty twice in one lifetime.

Chapter Three

Beth was alert the moment Dan's large hand gently touched her elbow. That worried her. She didn't like that she looked forward to the touch of a man she'd only just met.

"Careful. That floor is slick," he murmured.

She nodded, looking down at her stocking feet as she padded across the polished wood to the kitchen.

The closer they got, the stronger the enticing aromas grew. Yeasty warm bread and some sort of stew.

They entered the room and it was everything Beth would have imagined a farm kitchen should be. A humongous oval table with a cheery cotton tablecloth dominated the space. It was a table where a big family could gather and share meals, laughter and love.

The stove was modern, a stainless steel professional grade, and the double-door, brushed stainless steel refrigerator looked new. A braided rug in tones of burgundy and green covered the floor beneath the table and drew the colors of the room together.

Elsie pulled out a chair. "Have a seat, dear. You must be starving. It's been a long time since breakfast."

"GG, I want to sit next to Dr. Beth," Amy said.

"GG?" Beth asked.

"Oh, that's what Amy calls me. Grandma Gallagher is a mouthful, so she came up with that as soon as she learned the alphabet."

"GG and Pumpkin," Dan said.

Amy shot her father a tolerant glance.

"I'm saving this seat for you, Amy," Elsie said. She turned to Beth. "Coffee or tea? Or maybe hot cocoa?"

"Coffee would be lovely. Black. What can I do to help?"

"Sit, sit," Elsie said. "Everything is ready. You, too, Dan."

When he grabbed a chair at the other end of the table, his mother stopped him. "I'm sitting there. Do you mind? You can sit next to your guest."

The corners of Dan's mouth pulled upward slightly.

"Amy, you want to set the table?" Elsie asked as she slid steaming mugs of coffee in front of Beth and Dan.

"Sure, GG."

Elsie handed Amy burgundy quilted place mats and cloth napkins, along with silverware. Then she placed matching pottery plates and bowls in a stack on the table.

Amy concentrated on setting the table, a determined set to her little mouth.

"Nice job, Pumpkin," Dan said when she was done. He looked at Beth and winked. "Our Amy is the best table setter in the valley."

His daughter beamed at his praise. Dan was obviously a devoted father.

A father's love was instrumental in forming a young girl's sense of self-worth. Beth had learned that bit of information from a college psych class and she'd never forgotten the professor's words. It explained a lot, since in her case all she could remember were a couple of foster fathers who'd looked right through her with disinterest.

Elsie sat and gave a nod. Amy placed her tiny hand in Beth's left one and Dan took Beth's right hand in his large one. They all bowed their heads and Beth followed their motions.

Beth hadn't prayed over a meal since she'd been a senior in high school, living with Ben and his family. Yet this seemed so natural, so right. How could that be?

"Daniel, please lead us in prayer," Elsie said.

"Dear Lord, we thank You for the safety of this home. We ask You to take care of everyone out in the weather. We are thankful for this meal and ask You to bless this food to our bodies. Amen."

"Amen," Beth murmured.

Elsie jumped up after the prayer and ladled out the stew. When she offered Beth the basket of bread, Beth lifted her arm to reach for it, and grimaced.

"We need to check that shoulder," Dan said.

"It's not a big deal," she replied as she smoothed her napkin on her lap. "Hardly hurts at all now."

He raised a brow.

"Really. Besides, I heal extremely fast."

He laughed. "I bet you do. But you still need some ibuprofen and ice, Wonder Woman."

Beth arched a brow. She'd known the man four hours and already he knew how to push her buttons.

"Is Dr. Beth really Wonder Woman?" Amy asked, eyes wide.

"Daddy is kidding," Elsie answered, her lips twitching. "Right, Daddy?"

"Right."

"What happened to your shoulder?" Elsie asked.

"She fell," Dan explained.

"It's nothing," Beth insisted.

Dan raised his eyes from his meal to meet hers in a silent challenge.

"You really should have that checked, dear," Elsie admonished. "I'll get you an ice pack and some ibuprofen after we eat."

"Did I mention that Dr. Mom trumps a medical degree?" Dan said.

Beth suppressed a laugh.

"How's your stew?" Elsie asked.

"Delicious, thank you." Beth took another bite. It was good, savory and filling. Real food, not from a can, as was her usual fare.

"You're welcome. The beef is from our own ranch." Elsie looked at her. "Are you from Colorado?"

"I was born here, and I'm licensed in Colorado, but I haven't lived here in a very long time."

"And you're on your way to Gunbarrel," Elsie mused, as she buttered her bread and placed it on her plate. "Not much in Gunbarrel."

"It's halfway to the airport," Dan answered.

Elsie immediately looked up. "You're leaving? In the middle of a blizzard?" she exclaimed. "The weatherman says it's not going to stop snowing for another forty-eight hours. There's a second storm system moving in after midnight. Some sort of freak meteorological conditions. Why, they're saying we're going to break records."

"The weatherman has been known to be wrong," Dan stated.

Beth swallowed past the lump in her throat.

"Oh, I sincerely doubt it in this case," Elsie said.

Beth glanced at Dan, not missing the irony of the exchange. Hours ago he had made the same practical observation about the weather as his mother, but now he was offering Beth a tiny glimmer of hope. The gesture was kind, considering the reality she was faced with. Appetite waning, she stared unseeing at the remaining stew in the pottery bowl.

"Beth? Are you all right, dear?" Elsie probed gently.

"Yes. I'm sorry. I was supposed to start a new job Monday—that's why I needed to make my flight."

"Where is this job?" Elsie asked.

"A clinic in New York City."

"Oh, my. That's not good," she said. "Shall we pray about it? I know the good Lord is aware of the situation and has a solution in mind for you."

Beth had trouble meeting the older woman's eyes. "No, but thank you." She doubted the Lord cared about her job interview. He was busy taking care of important things, like people stranded in this blizzard.

"We've got a landline," Elsie added. "Perhaps you should try to leave a message for that clinic in New York soon, in case we lose the phones in the storm."

"That's a good idea. Thank you," Beth said.

"By the way, I called Ben and Sara to let them know you're safe, and staying here with us," Dan interjected. "But I bet they'd like to hear from you."

Beth nodded and met his eyes. He was a thoughtful man and he was right, of course. She should have thought of calling Ben, but she wasn't accustomed to checking in with anyone.

"You look exhausted," Elsie observed. "I'll wrap up your stew and we'll save it for later. Okay?" She looked to her son. "Show Beth the guest room, won't you, Dan?"

After stopping in the hall to grab her tote bag and coat, Dan led her to the other side of the big house. The Gallagher home was warm and friendly and it seemed to have been updated recently. The paint was fresh and the furniture new. Comfortable oak pieces filled the living room, and the burgundy-and-green color palette ran through the house. It was a no-fuss place that welcomed friends, family, children, grandchildren and very enthusiastic dogs.

"I want to apologize for my behavior this morning," Beth said as she followed Dan down the hall.

"What behavior?" he asked, moving her tote from one hand to the other.

"Are you kidding? I was freaking out."

"Totally normal."

"Not for me. Not ever," she said.

"Look, you can lose control with me anytime."

They both stopped in their tracks.

Dan's ears were red as he slowly turned around, and she could see the appalled expression on his face.

Beth couldn't help herself. She burst out laughing. The humor of the situation eased the tension she'd been wearing like a heavy coat all day. For the first time in hours, she relaxed.

"You know what I mean," he said firmly.

"I do." She smiled. "Thank you for getting me to your house, and for trusting me to meet your family."

He nodded, and despite his stern expression, the corners of his mouth threatened to curve into a grin and his eyes sparkled with humor.

"Dan, the CB is going off. You'll want to see to that," Elsie called out as she came down the hall with a medicine bottle and an ice pack. "I'll get Beth settled in."

"Thanks." He turned to Beth and gave a nod. "I'll leave you in the good hands of Dr. Mom."

Beth continued to smile as she watched him walk away, then she hurried her steps to catch up with Elsie.

Elsie opened a door at the end of the hall. "There are three bedrooms upstairs and this is the only one downstairs. When the kids were living at home they shared. My husband always said that sharing a room builds character. My kids are characters, so I suppose he was right." She chuckled at her own words.

Before Beth could respond, Elsie turned on the light and then handed her the ibuprofen and ice pack. "Here we go."

An antique, wrought-iron bed occupied most of

the space. A thick duvet in a peach-and-rose-colored paisley covered it.

"What a welcoming room," Beth said.

"Yes. Nice and toasty, being on the ground floor. Though not as quiet as upstairs." Elsie walked directly across the hall. "Private bathroom. Plenty of towels and anything else you might need in the closet. I just stocked the drawers for you with shampoo and whatnot." She grinned. "Girlie stuff. I keep a supply of it for when my daughters come home."

"Thank you, so much," Beth said, truly touched by the kind gestures.

"Oh, no problem. It's fun to have company, and especially nice to have another woman around."

"Thank you."

Elsie looked at Beth, her expression sympathetic. "I'm so sorry about your job. But I will be sure to add you to my prayer list during my prayer time in the morning. And I want you to remember that God has a plan for you, Beth."

"I hope so," she murmured.

"No hoping about God. Trust me on this. After all, you don't raise four children and bury a husband without learning a bit about the nature of the good Lord. He loves you so much He gathers your sorrows and collects your tears. Did you know that?"

"No, I didn't." Beth pondered the words, finding herself intrigued by the comment.

Elsie smiled. "Absolutely true. Now, you help

yourself to anything you want. The refrigerator is open 24/7. I'm working on a quilt in the sewing room, other side of the kitchen. If you need anything feel free to come and find me."

"Okay." She paused. "Mrs. Gallagher?"

"Yes?"

"Thanks very much."

Elsie cocked her head. "For what, dear?"

"Welcoming me into your home," Beth said.

"You're very welcome. And you can call me Elsie."

Beth nodded and slowly closed the door behind Dan's mother. She sank into the peach Parsons chair next to the dresser and dug in her tote for her phone, punching in her cousin's number.

"Hey, Beth. Dan called to let us know what happened. He said you're staying at his mother's."

"Yes."

"Elsie is a hoot, isn't she?"

"She is." Beth released a short laugh "Actually, all of the Gallaghers that I've met are nice. I like them."

"They're good folk."

"So, is everything okay at your place?" Beth asked.

"Yeah. We lost power, but I have a couple backup generators. That snow plays havoc on the trees and then they hit those wires, so we're used to dealing with it."

"Could that happen here?"

"Elsie has generators, too. Everyone does up here. You're safe."

Beth glanced around the cozy room. *Safe.*

"Are you okay, Beth?" Ben asked. "You sound… off."

"Yes. I'm fine."

"Remember, everything is going to work out."

"Do you think so?"

"I do. Beth, this storm is huge. It's on all the national news channels. Storm of the year, they're calling it. That practice in New York will realize soon enough that there was nothing you could do to get there."

"I hope you're right. I'll leave a message with them and then try to reach someone through the answering service in the morning."

"Good." He paused. "And, Beth, Dan is a good guy. You can trust him."

"Will I need to?"

"You have to trust someone."

"I'll give that some thought. Thanks, Ben. I'll check in with you tomorrow. Tell Sara and the babies hello."

"I will."

Beth punched in the number of the clinic. The out-of-office voice mail message droned in her ear, advising her that the clinic was closed and offering her the number for the emergency doctor on call.

Frustrated, she put the phone down, then plugged

in the charger and turned off the volume. She'd call again later. Leaning back against the soft padding of the chair, she stared out the window at the still-falling snow.

Her glance moved to the worn leather Bible on the oak bureau. She got up and put the book on the bed, flipping through the pages. What had Elsie said?

God has a plan for you.

"I certainly hope He'll let me in on the plan soon."

Dan looked up as one of the garage's big doors swung open, blowing in a gust of wind and snow flurries along with his mother.

"Everything okay?" he asked.

Elsie shut the door and then pushed off her hood. "Yes. Your guest is resting." She stomped the snow from her boots. "Amy is coloring. I gave her the walkie-talkie."

He nodded. "Quiet is good, right?"

"Mmm-hmm," she replied.

Dan continued his task of checking supplies in the storage compartments of the snowmobile and restocking his emergency medical tackle box. It was routine to have everything ready to go for the next emergency call.

Elsie walked around the building, stopping to examine the vehicles. She lifted the tarp on Joe's brand-new oversize pickup. The truck had been put away since the accident. Joe couldn't handle the gearshift after he lost his right arm.

"Will Joe be able to change gears in his truck with the prosthesis?" Elsie asked.

"Sure. He'll learn how. Remember, he's going to have occupational therapy. Until then he can use his old automatic truck."

"Think he'll follow through with therapy?"

"I think Joe will do anything he has to, in order to get his life back to normal."

"I hope you're right."

She wandered over to examine the on-call calendar tacked to the wall.

"Need anything in particular?" Dan asked.

"No. Just came out to chat."

Dan's ears perked up. He sensed trouble coming. "Chat" was code for his mother trying to ferret out information he was not interested in dispensing.

"So," Elsie continued. "Beth certainly is a surprise, isn't she?"

Dan froze for a moment before he raised the brim of his hat to better assess his mother. Yep. She was on a mission. "A surprise?" he slowly asked, keeping his voice void of emotion.

"I just mean she's such a sweet girl. And so pretty. Did you notice?"

Did he notice? A mental picture of Beth's dimples and soft blue eyes distracted him from his mother's words for a moment. He shook his head, bringing himself back to reality. That reality was that he liked his life just the way it was.

"She's on her way to New York," he said flatly.

"Oh, I know." His mother's tone was musing and Dan shivered.

Silence stretched.

"It's been six years and you haven't even been on a date," Elsie observed.

Dan sighed. Okay, well at least now they were on familiar ground. The same old story he heard week in and week out. "I have a daughter to think about."

"Oh, pooh, Amy isn't the issue here."

"What is the issue here?" he returned.

"You."

Dan said nothing for a long moment. He didn't think he was gun-shy. Sure, he'd made a mistake six years ago, but he'd learned plenty since then. He'd like nothing more than to settle down in Paradise with someone special. That someone special just hadn't come along yet.

His mother meant well, but he didn't have the energy or desire for a debate. "I'm thinking that if you want to fix someone you should take care of Joe. He's got a chip on his shoulder bigger than the valley."

His mother paused and tilted her head, eyes narrowing. "True. One project at a time."

Dan bent down for a final check of the supplies, and then stood and dusted off his hands.

"What's next?" Elsie asked.

"I've already looked in on the cattle and brought a few pregnant heifers into the barn."

"Problems?"

"I don't know, but they were acting strange, so I want to keep a closer eye on them. I'll check them again during the night."

"What's the feed situation?"

"I'm about to put out the hay and feed cakes."

"I can help."

"You've covered for me all morning. Take a break, Mom."

"I merely fed the chickens and the herd dogs. Even Amy can handle that."

"That's one less thing for me to do."

"I'll help with the cattle," she said.

Dan exhaled and faced his mother. "You don't trust me to do Joe's job?"

"Of course I do. All I'm saying is that ranch work is safer in pairs. Everyone knows that. Look at your brother. If he'd only waited for you…" His mother's lips thinned, and for a brief moment her shoulders sagged with grief for her eldest son.

Dan couldn't deny her logic there. If Joe had waited for him to help with that tractor repair he might not have lost his arm. But Dan wasn't going there. Not today. He'd just end up feeling guilty over something that wasn't his fault. Joe was stubborn and that wasn't going to change anytime soon.

He moved to his mother's side and gave her a long hug. "Look, I promise to call the house when I need help."

"Thank you," she whispered.

The landline began to ring and Dan reached for the receiver, grateful for the interruption.

"Hey, Ben. Okay, got the situation covered. Yeah, no problem. I'll keep you in the loop and we'll be praying."

His mother raised her brows, concern on her face.

"Ben's at the Paradise Hospital. Deke Andrews's dad fell on the ice and broke a hip."

"Oh, no. What's the situation?"

"On his way into surgery. Maybe you better call the Paradise Ladies Auxiliary and tell them to start the prayer chain."

"Yes. Yes. I'll do that." She frowned. "So does that mean you're on call again?"

"Deke was covering for me. Now call duty is mine again. You can add the ranch to your prayer list, as well, because if those cows start calving early and I get called out on a medical emergency you might find yourself helping out with more than you signed on for."

Elsie merely grinned, excited as a kid. "Just like the old days. I used to help your father when calving season began."

"I'm glad you're happy, because I keep thinking about all the potentials for disaster. Every cow counts, as Joe always says, and he's not going to understand if I leave the ranch to tend to a mere human when his precious cows are calving."

"You can only do your best."

"I hope my best is good enough. Joe's been through enough. I don't want to let him down now."

"I'm proud of you, Dan, and I know Joe will be, as well. Just remember you aren't in this alone. The Lord is on your side, and so am I."

Dan shook his head as his mother's words sank in. "You're right, Mom. I'm not alone." He smiled. "How'd you get to be so smart?"

Elsie merely grinned.

Chapter Four

The house was quiet as Dan tucked his flannel shirt into his jeans and crossed the living room toward the kitchen. Barely 6:00 a.m. The sun wouldn't rise for another hour, but there was way too much to do and he was restless.

He started the coffee, and as the brewer gurgled and then hissed, he pulled two muffins out of the fridge and began a mental list of the day's chores. His gaze drifted to the big picture window. Snow continued to fall; now forming drifts that hugged the barn and the garage. The moonlight illuminated the sky, and he could make out the dark humps that were actually cattle huddled together in the feeding pen.

"Coffee." The whispered word was as earnest as a prayer.

Dan turned to see Beth in the doorway. She barely acknowledged him as she sank into a kitchen chair.

"Addiction problem?" he murmured.

"Yes. My only vice."

"Only one vice?"

The corner of her mouth quirked, but her eyelids remained at half-mast. "That I will readily admit to."

"Ah." He nodded. "Don't like it fancy, I hope."

"No. Just strong."

"That I can do." Dan pulled two stoneware mugs from the cupboard and set them on the counter.

"What about you?" she asked.

He raised his brows.

"No vices?"

"Salted caramels."

Her eyes opened and her brows rose in surprise before she released a short laugh.

"Those soft, melt-in-your-mouth ones that are sprinkled with sea salt," Dan explained.

"I would have never guessed."

"Now you know my secret. I hope I can count on your discretion."

Beth crossed her heart with a finger and nodded.

Dan smiled and couldn't help appraising the city girl. Today her hair was swept back, away from her face in a no-fuss ponytail, low on her neck. He didn't know much about makeup, but her face didn't look to be made up.

She wore plain, ordinary jeans, not even the skinny kind, and a bulky forest-green sweater that fell to her hips and concealed her figure. Obviously, she was more comfort-focused than fashion conscious.

Points for her.

"How's your shoulder?" he asked.

"The patient is much improved."

"Hmm" was his muttered response.

She pinned him with her gaze. "Do I sense doubt at my qualified medical opinion?"

"Full range of motion?" he countered, ignoring her comment.

"Partial, and the pain *is* significantly diminished."

Dan nodded and poured the coffee. "Black, right?"

"Yes. Thanks."

"Did you get a call through to New York?" he asked as he slid into a chair across from her.

"Interesting segue," she said as she took a sip of coffee.

Dan smiled and wrapped his hands around his mug, waiting.

"I did get in touch with the on-call physician after a few tries, and he was very understanding. I've rescheduled my flight for Thursday afternoon. That will give me some time to relax before the Friday morning interview."

"That's positive thinking."

She blinked. "You don't think I can get to New York by Thursday night?"

"The truth?"

"Always."

"Could be, but you might have saved yourself some stress by making it for the following Monday."

"No. They'd have replaced me for certain if I couldn't get there before then."

"Do you honestly want an employer who values you so little they'll hold the weather against you?"

Beth didn't answer. She stared down at her coffee, finally lifting the mug and taking another sip.

"You said you wanted the truth," he murmured.

"And you're very good at that," Beth returned with a tight smile.

"Muffin?" Dan offered. He slid a plate with a plump, golden muffin across the table, along with a napkin.

"Peace offering?" she asked.

Taken off guard by her response, Dan laughed and shook his head. "Maybe."

Beth peeled the paper off her muffin and broke it in half. "What are these?"

"My mother calls them kitchen sink muffins. Fruit, nuts and seeds. They stick to you, that's for sure."

She took a bite. "Good stuff."

He noted her long, slim fingers as she picked up crumbs from the table. No rings, and while her nails were polished, they were short and practical. Even the color, a pale pink, was simple and subdued.

The woman was a puzzle. She gave away very

little, yet her panic in the truck had been very real and didn't mesh with the no-nonsense, controlled woman with the quirky sense of humor who sat across from him. He pondered that as he ate his own muffin.

There was an intimacy in the quiet meal they shared. It was pleasant, and he couldn't help but wonder what it would be like to share breakfast each day with someone like Beth.

Her gaze met his and she quickly looked away, her face coloring and her lashes fluttering in apparent confusion. Her attention quickly moved to the view outside the window.

Was she having the same thoughts?

Dan studied her profile, admiring the smooth column of her neck visible above the sweater's rolled collar. A few tendrils of hair had escaped her ponytail and rested on her ear.

Yes, she was beautiful, but what did he really know about Beth Rogers? Experience had taught him the hard way that you didn't really get to know someone when things were going fine. Reality poked up its head when you least expected it—usually when your guard was down. When the going was rough. Yeah, that was when you really discovered a person's mettle.

The wall phone began to ring and Dan grabbed it before the sound woke the entire household.

"Gallagher." He paused. "Okay. Tell Abel to

relax, I'm on my way." Dan shook his head and put the receiver back in the cradle.

"Everything okay?"

"Looks like I'm going to deliver a baby today. Midwife can't get through."

"Have you ever delivered a baby?" Beth asked.

He shrugged. "Naw, but there's no better time to learn than the present. Besides, Ben is the doctor on call. He'll meet me there."

"Why bother Ben when I'm sitting around doing nothing?"

"You *want* to go?"

Beth nodded.

Elsie strolled into the kitchen, her eyes curious. A pleased smile crossed her face when she spotted Beth and Dan. Today his mother's sweatshirt was buttercup-yellow and bore the words I May Be Wrong, But I Doubt It.

"Go where?" she asked.

"Home birth and Emily can't get through."

"You'll have to take Beth. She's a doctor and you've never delivered a baby."

Dan barely resisted groaning. *Thank you, Mother.* He could count on Elsie to reduce him to the youngest child in a heartbeat.

Beth's eyes met his and she bit her lip as though undecided as to whether she should weigh in on the discussion. "I'm happy to assist," she finally said. "Your decision."

"I can do the ranch chores while you're gone," Elsie added as she poured herself a cup of coffee.

"What about Amy?" Dan asked.

"Amy and Millie can go with me, and I'll bring her back when she's tired." Elsie's eyes widened and she smiled. "Oh, and I'll take Joe's new truck. It'll get through the snow on the ranch road."

Dan grimaced.

"Now who's having trust issues?" his mother said with an appraising glance.

"I'm just saying, you know how Joe is about that truck."

"Pshaw. Now, what do you want us to do?"

"Check the cows and lay out the hay and feed. Oh, and Joe's herd dogs are in the barn. They'll want some exercise. And my horses. Stalls need attention, too." Again Dan looked out the window. "Sure you're up to this?"

Elsie put her hands on her hips. "Who do you think did the chores when there were no kids around here?"

"Uh, Dad?" he offered.

"Why is it so hard for you to believe that your father and I did them together? We were a team."

Dan did the math. Joe was the eldest and he was thirty-two. Probably not a good idea to remind his mother that she was talking about thirty odd years ago. Instead, he cleared his throat and looked at

Beth, effectively changing the subject. "What's your specialty?"

"Internal medicine."

"Delivered any babies?"

"Not since medical school. I let the OB docs do that."

"Isn't it just like riding a bike?" Elsie countered.

"Ah, not quite," Beth answered.

"Better eat up," Dan told her. "I've got a few more supplies to load in the snowmobile and then we're heading out. There's no telling when we'll be back."

"How far away is it?" she asked.

"Short stroll up the road."

Beth's lips parted and then she paused, a confused frown on her face.

"What?" Dan asked, nearly laughing out loud.

"I'm having a difficult time translating 'up the road' and 'not far.' Apparently they don't mean the same thing to you as they do to me."

"You've got that right." Elsie's laughter trilled out.

"Can I go?" a pajama-clad Amy asked from the doorway. Millie stood at her side, eagerly inspecting the floor. The mutt lived in the hope that crumbs would appear.

"May I." Elsie corrected. "Sorry, sweetie, but there's only room for two on the snowmobile. Daddy certainly isn't going to let Dr. Beth walk in this weather."

"I was kidding about the stroll." Dan pulled out

a chair for his daughter and brushed her hair out of her face. "Amy, what are you doing up so early?" He glanced around. "What are you all doing up so early?"

"The phone woke me," Amy said.

"I've been awake for hours, just praying," Elsie stated, gazing out the window at the cows. "My joints ache when the barometer drops." She turned to Beth. "They say that the low barometric pressure makes the cows drop calves early, too."

"I didn't know that," she said.

"Am I right, Dan?" his mother asked.

Dan glanced at the wall clock and then back to the room full of females. Beth, his mother, Amy, and even Millie were all looking at him.

"You are right as always, Mother. Now, I think that Dr. Rogers and I have a baby to deliver, and we had better get going. You could start praying that the barometer doesn't affect those heifers while I'm gone, or we're going to be in big trouble."

Beth swiped at the wet flakes on her goggles with a gloved hand. Snow continued to fall as Dan led the snowmobile to their destination "up the road," which took nearly an hour. But despite the weather, she didn't mind the long trip. Riding the snowmobile was no longer scary, and if pushed, she might even admit she enjoyed riding tandem with the tall cowboy.

When they arrived at the log cabin deep in the woods, above the town of Paradise, another snow-mobile was already there. A huge, cherry-red snow-mobile with flame detailing along the sides.

A tall, blond and bearded mountain of a man greeted them at the door.

"Abel," Dan said as he grabbed the tackle box and approached the house. "This is Dr. Rogers."

The big man frowned, his bushy eyebrows knit in confusion. "Another Dr. Rogers?"

Dan laughed. "Yeah."

"Nice to meet you, ma'am." The giant stuck out a hand. "I'm Abel Frank."

"Nice to meet you, too," Beth returned. Her small hand was swallowed whole in a gentle grip.

Dan glanced at the snowmobile parked next to his own. "Deke? I thought his father was in the hospital."

"He is. Emily Robbs made it in on his machine."

Dan's eyes widened and he sputtered. "He lent Big Red to Emily?"

"Tell me about it." Abel shrugged. "Apparently Deke's sweet on Emily."

Dan shook his head. "Unbelievable."

Seriously? They sounded like sixteen-year-olds instead of grown men. Beth cleared her throat.

Both Dan and Abel turned, their expressions sheepish, before they looked back at each other.

Dan opened his mouth, then closed it again.

"Uh, why don't you come in?" Abel said. "Contractions are pretty close together now. I'm guessing we're going to have a baby real soon."

He held the door as Dan and Beth stepped into the huge home.

"You're awfully calm for a man whose wife is about to have a baby," Beth observed.

"This is our sixth and I don't have to help."

"That's a good thing?" she asked.

"Oh, yeah. I can't stomach the sight of blood."

"Where are the kids?" Dan asked. "This place is way too quiet."

"They spent the night at their grandparents' in Gunbarrel. Mom decided my wife needed a break to get things in order before the delivery. Now Grams and Gramps are stranded with five kids. Good timing, I'd say."

Dan chuckled.

"Go on down the hall." Abel pointed left. "Excuse me while I grab more towels and ice chips."

Beth glanced around. The two-story structure had high ceilings and a loft above the great room. The words *log cabin* hardly applied to the spacious home decorated in a Western theme, though it *was* entirely made of logs. She had a difficult time believing five children lived here, because nothing was out of place.

"Dan, is that you?"

Beth noted the familiarity in the woman's voice.

"Yes, ma'am. Okay to come in?" he called.

"Absolutely. Moral support is always welcome."

Dan entered the room first, a wide grin on his face.

A vivacious and lean strawberry blonde in baby blue scrubs stood next to a cast-iron, king-size bed. She held a fetal Doppler to the abdomen of a petite woman whose dark hair was piled on her head. The bed's top sheet was tented over the pregnant woman's propped up knees.

The even and rhythmic sound of the baby's heartbeat echoed in the room from the ultrasound speaker.

"Hey, Emily. How's your patient?" Dan asked, with a wink to the woman in the bed.

"Ha. The patient. I'm between contractions. Thanks for asking. Did you bring me chocolate?"

"Oops. I clean forgot."

The blonde, who had to be the Emily Dan and Abel had mentioned, crossed the room and wrapped her arms around Dan in a warm hug. The woman's smile was almost intimate and Beth looked away, surprised at the kick of jealousy rising in her.

Of course women were attracted to Dan Gallagher, she told herself. He was a handsome man. A nice man, as well. More important, he was merely an acquaintance in her world, and his relationship with Emily was none of her business.

When the midwife glanced over Dan's shoulder

and met Beth's gaze, her eyes widened a fraction, and she stepped away.

"Oh, hi. I didn't realize Dan brought a friend." She looked into his face. "We go back a long way, right, pal?"

"Uh, yeah. Kindergarten. Emily, this is Dr. Elizabeth Rogers." He turned to Beth. "Beth, meet Emily Robbs, midwife, and Karen Frank, chocoholic."

Karen smiled and then flinched, her hands gripping the sides of her large, round abdomen. "Nice to meet you. I'd get up, but I don't think I can."

"Dr. Rogers?" Emily said with a lift of her brows.

"Ben is my cousin."

"Oh. I didn't realize he had any family in the area." She moved back to the bed. "Roll, honey, and I'll give that lower back a good massage."

"I'm just here visiting," Beth answered. "I was waylaid by the storm."

"Nice of you to come out in this weather." Emily gave her a sincere smile before her gaze slid to Dan. "Have you known Dan a long time?"

"No, not very long," Beth answered.

"I thought you couldn't get through. Mind explaining how you managed to wrangle Deke's snowmobile?" Dan asked.

Emily applied a washcloth to Karen's forehead. "Wrangle? I like to think of it as a negotiation."

Dan laughed. "Oh, boy. Maybe I don't want to

know the details." His expression became serious. "How's his dad?"

"I called before I got here. He's out of surgery. No complications."

"Glad to hear that."

"When did you arrive?" Dan asked.

"About forty-five minutes ago. At first I wasn't sure I was going to make it, even with Deke's beast machine, but God was with me all the way."

He looked at Karen. "What's the status of our mother here?"

The midwife grabbed latex gloves from a box at the bedside. "She began labor during the night and things are moving along pretty quickly. The pregnancy has been unremarkable, so we don't anticipate any problems."

"All the other births were at home, weren't they?" Dan asked.

Karen nodded. "Yes. Apparently, I pop them out like gum balls, although this one is moving even faster than my other babies, and according to Emily..." Karen swallowed "...he's breech."

"Breech?" Dan's voice went up an octave.

"Relax," Emily said. "We managed to coax little Oscar into a more appropriate presentation."

"But it wasn't easy. He's stubborn, like his father," Karen added. "We prayed. A lot."

"Have I mentioned how glad I am you're here?" Dan said to Emily.

She grinned. "I'm glad you're here, too, sweetie. Just remember that the next time I call and ask you to take me to the Founder's Day Supper." She glanced at her watch. "Should be starting again, Karen?"

Karen nodded and gripped Emily's hand. "Ooh, I think this is it. I really think this is it. *He's coming now.*"

"Easy, Karen. Yes. He's crowning. I see a dark scalp. Lots of hair, too."

"Here you go. More ice chips and towels," Abel announced. Beth and Dan turned when he strode into the room at the exact moment his wife pushed, and the baby's head and shoulders appeared.

"Good girl, Karen. Once more and we'll have our baby boy," Emily said.

Abel's face paled and his eyes rolled back. The big man dropped the glass and towels as he crumpled like a house of cards.

Dan raced toward him, but not fast enough. Abel landed with a thud, right on the broken glass.

"Abel!" Karen screeched.

The cries of a newborn tangled with her scream.

"I've got him, Karen," Dan said.

He rolled Abel over to his side, and using the dropped towels, brushed the large piece of glass Abel had landed on out of the way.

"Can you tear that fabric away from his back so we can examine him?" Beth asked.

"Tackle box. Top drawer. Scissors," Dan said.

Abel moaned.

"Gloves?" Beth asked.

"Right drawer."

She pulled out two packages and tossed one to Dan before pulling on her own.

"I've got him," she said, as she held Abel's torso so Dan could tug on his gloves and slice through the blood-soaked shirt.

When he was done, he grabbed saline and sterile gauze and placed them next to her.

Beth leaned forward. "Suture kit?"

"Got it."

"What?" Abel said, trying to get up.

"Hold still, Dad," Dan commanded, with a hand on the big man's shoulder. "Let us clean this up and you can meet your son."

"Any allergies?" Beth asked.

"None," Abel groaned.

Dan held Abel firmly as Beth doused the area with sterile saline and carefully picked out smaller bits of glass with forceps. Then she swabbed the area with Betadine.

Anticipating her needs, Dan filled a syringe with lidocaine, before opening the suture kit and placing the contents on a sterile field.

Beth injected the anesthetic on both sides of the wound, and then began putting in stitches. Six sutures later and the wound edges were approximated. Satisfied, she laid the knot down flat and then dressed the site.

"Nice work," Dan commented.

"Thank you," she murmured.

"You need to ask my mother to teach you to needlepoint. You're a natural."

She chuckled and their eyes met and held. Her face warmed.

"Can I see?" Abel asked.

"Let me get you a mirror," Beth said.

"Not my back, Doc. I want to see my baby." Abel slowly sat up and then stood, leaning on Dan.

Emily laughed. "Your son is ready for you."

Karen smiled from the bed, where she lay propped against a pillow, a small bundle in a blue blanket cradled in her arms.

"So this is what your rescue team is all about," Beth said quietly to Dan.

"Not always such happy endings, but there's not a day that I'm not glad I'm doing the work God intended for me to be doing."

"God intended," Beth repeated.

"Yeah. It's definitely a calling. A ministry."

She pondered his words.

"We could use someone like you on the team," Dan murmured.

Beth met his gaze and paused. His smile caught her and she lost focus, lured for a brief, reckless moment into considering a future outside of her carefully laid plans.

Dan Gallagher stirred something in her that she wasn't familiar with. For the very first time in her entire life, she was tempted to consider acting from her feelings instead of her head.

She averted her gaze and rational thought once again took over. Paradise was, after all, merely a stop on the road to her tomorrow. Dan Gallagher a pleasant detour. That was the reality she had to cling to.

Chapter Five

Nearly 11:00 a.m. on a Sunday and there was no traffic anywhere between Abel and Karen Frank's cabin and home.

The ride was eerily quiet, as though the rest of the world had disappeared. The storm continued to steadily dump thick snow on the valley. Anyone who lived in Paradise awhile knew that the best thing to do when Mother Nature raged was to lie low and wait her out. It was safer for everyone that way.

The snowmobile plowed on without incident. For that, Dan was grateful.

Arriving at the ranch, he slid from his seat and held out a hand to Beth.

She gripped it easily, the action as natural as the falling flakes. He had to admit there was something that felt right about Beth becoming more and more comfortable around him.

"We're going to check on Karen and Abel and

the baby tomorrow, right?" Beth queried. "I mean, there's really no need for Emily to go out again when we can check everyone when we follow up with Abel's incision, right?"

"You're the doctor," Dan said.

"What do you think?" she asked, tucking her helmet beneath her arm like an old pro. Beth neither realized nor seemed to care that her hair was flat and tangled and her mascara smudged.

It only made her more attractive in his estimation. Dangerously so. Dan averted his gaze.

"Good plan," he said. "Unless the cows start delivering, or we're needed for a real emergency call."

"Oh," she said, crinkling her brow in thought. "I hadn't considered that."

"No big deal. This was a field call. You're still on an adrenaline rush."

Beth hesitated for a moment before continuing. "Are you and Emily, um, close?" Her cheeks flooded with color. "I mean, it's none of my business, but I didn't want her to think you and I…" Her voice trailed off and she glanced away.

Dr. Elizabeth Rogers was embarrassed? "We're only friends," he assured her. "Since kindergarten."

"Right. Yes. You said that." She nodded and headed toward the house, then stopped and turned. "Aren't you coming in?"

"Going to check on the cattle."

"May I help?" she asked.

"You've probably had enough fun for one day."

"I'm not used to sitting around, and you're right, I'm still pretty wound up."

"Okay, but don't say I didn't warn you." He put his helmet back on. "We'll take the four-wheeler to the barn."

Once they were outside the barn door Joe's two border collie herd dogs enthusiastically greeted them. Dan slid through the open door and signaled for Beth to follow. Inside, Elsie stood, hands on hips, staring at the backside of a pregnant cow.

"What's going on?" Dan asked.

Elsie whirled around. "Dan. Thank goodness. Never a dull moment at the Gallagher Ranch," she said.

He nodded toward the cow. "What's the story?"

"This poor thing wants to deliver," Elsie said, propping a hand on the rough-hewn wood stall. "She's been pacing and pacing, and her water still hasn't broken."

"How long has this been going on?"

"About an hour and a half."

"Time to give her some help." Dan cautiously glanced around the barn. "What other problems?"

"I had a delivery while you were gone," Elsie said with a proud grin.

"Did you?" He shook his head. "Everything go okay?"

Elsie's grin widened. "Yes. Twins."

"*Whoa!* You delivered twins?"

Elsie laughed. "Believe me, I was as surprised as you are. But the truth is, that cow didn't want or need my help. Imagine that."

"Someone was watching over you," Dan said.

"I have extra prayers stocked up in a reserve tank," his mother returned.

"I guess so," Dan said with a laugh.

"The momma and babies are in the far stall. The last time I checked, momma was acknowledging only one of her babies," Elsie said.

Dan ran a hand over his face. "I'd say calving season has officially begun."

"How long is calving season?" Beth asked.

"For us, around thirty to sixty days. Joe only has about two hundred head," he said. Beth nodded. "Where's Amy?" Dan asked, with another glance around the barn.

"She was exhausted after getting up so early. I gave her lunch and she's taking a nap now." Elsie held up a walkie-talkie. "The other one is next to her, and Millie is at the house as well."

"Thanks, Mom."

"My pleasure. Contrary to popular opinion, I still have what it takes," she said.

"I never doubted you for a minute," Dan said.

"Ha!" Elsie zipped up her coat and then fished in her pockets for her mittens and put them on.

"Why don't you go in the house? You're freezing," Dan said.

"I was fine when I was running around, but now that you're here to take care of things, I think I will. I could use a nap, too." She glanced at her watch. "It's been an hour since my last check of the pen."

"Thanks." He put a hand on his mother's arm. "Seriously, Mom, you really did a great job."

"You're welcome. I'll bring you back a colostrum bottle for that twin." Elsie pulled up the hood on her coat. "Oh, and I forgot to ask. How did your call go?"

"Emily arrived just before us," Dan said.

"I imagine you were relieved," his mother stated.

"Yeah, and Beth got to suture up Abel. So it was worth the trip."

"Abel hurt himself?"

"He fainted and ended up with a laceration requiring stitches," Beth added.

"Oh, my."

When Dan headed to the far side of the barn to retrieve a pitchfork, Elsie closed in on Beth.

"How did you like Emily?" Elsie murmured.

The barn acoustics were excellent and Dan didn't miss a single word of the inquisition.

"She was nice," Beth said.

"Emily is crazy about Dan," Elsie whispered. "Almost as crazy about Dan as Deke is over the moon for Emily," she added.

"Oh?" was all Beth said in reply.

"My eye is twitching," Dan called as he prepared the hay in another stall. "Are you talking about me?"

"That's not how it goes." His mother laughed. "If your right ear itches, someone is talking bad about you. If your left ear itches, someone who cares about you is thinking about you."

"Hmm," Dan said. "You didn't answer my question."

Elsie laughed again. "Didn't I?"

Dan led the pregnant heifer to the new stall and gently directed her into the head gate. The metal gate clanged shut around her, holding her in position. He patted her chocolate-brown hide and began to soothe the heifer. "Time for delivery, little momma."

"And time for me to go," his own mother announced. "I've had my share of childbirth for the day." Elsie looked to Beth. "Do you want to come in the house? We've got hot cocoa."

"I'd like to stay," Beth replied.

"It might not be pleasant," Elsie warned.

"I can handle unpleasant."

Elsie cocked her head and offered another one of her knowing smiles. "I'm sure you can."

As if to test the good doctor's comment, the moment the door closed behind Elsie, the cow's water sac broke. Beth jumped back and tensed.

"You okay?" Dan asked.

"Of course. I…I just haven't been around animals very much."

"I thought you and Ben were raised in the country."

"I only lived with Ben a short time."

"Oh, I guess I thought you two grew up together." He slipped on a clear glove that reached his shoulder, and lubricated his right hand.

"Are you checking the positioning?" Beth asked.

"Yeah." The cow moved in agitation as Dan probed her. Satisfied, he removed the glove. "The baby is fine." He looked to Beth. "Want to hold that tail out of the way for me? Toward you."

She grabbed the tail and held it aside as Dan fastened chains on the protruding calf hooves. If Beth was nervous, she hid her emotions well. He reached for a U-shaped contraption.

"What's that?"

"Brace. I'll use the ratchet to ease the baby out, nice and low, like the momma would if she was pushing the way she ought to be."

Dan gritted his teeth and pulled, his knees locked until he was nearly sitting on the ground. Finally, the dark rocket of a calf slid from her momma and into the hay. Dan grabbed the calf by the legs and moved her, releasing the chain. Then he gently stimulated the animal's throat and cleared the fluid from the nose. A dark, wide eye appeared and then another. The calf took a gulping breath.

"Yes!" Dan shouted in triumph.

Beth released a breath, as well.

Dan's gaze met hers and he smiled. "Pretty good show, huh?"

A smile touched the corners of her mouth and her eyes lit up as she nodded.

Dan lifted the little calf by her spindly legs over to the clean stall, then unfastened the momma cow and led her to her baby.

Arms resting on the top of the wooden stall fence, he and Beth watched the new family settle in.

"Something sort of basic about all this, isn't there?" Dan asked.

"How do you mean?" She turned to him.

"I don't know. This and Karen's birth today. Sort of levels everything down to the most common denominator. Makes you evaluate why we're here."

Beth's blue eyes were clear as they met his. "It's a different world from what I'm used to," she finally said.

"Yeah, it's a *real* world, although I'll be the first to admit that I didn't always appreciate that. There was a time when all I wanted was to get out of Paradise."

"Oh?"

"Long story short—I went away to college and decided I wasn't coming back. I begged my father to buy me out of my portion of the ranch." Dan's lips were thin as he admitted the truth, which still hurt after all these years. "He did, even though he knew I was making the biggest mistake of my life."

"But you came back."

"Yeah. The prodigal son returned. With a baby in one hand and my PharmD in the other. My father was dying and I realized too late that I needed to be with my family. Amy's mother didn't share my revelation."

"She left?"

"Yeah. That was a painful time for all of us." Dan paused and looked away. "I, ah, I haven't talked about this to anyone in a long time."

"Maybe you needed to."

"I guess." His gaze met hers. "Sometimes I forget how fortunate I am."

"A loving family makes all the difference."

"Don't I know it? They were there for me and when the dust settled everything turned out all right. The best part is I'm happy and so is Amy." He reached for a bottle of disinfectant.

"You're a good father," Beth murmured.

Dan looked up as he cleaned his hands. "You barely know me. How can you be so sure?"

She shrugged. "Reading people accurately is a survival skill that I learned at a young age."

"Survival?" Dan asked as he moved to the next stall to check on another heifer. "Is that why you're so guarded?"

Beth drew back and stared at him. "I'm not guarded. Cautious maybe." She crossed her arms.

"Isn't that the same thing?"

"No," she said.

"Hmm." He knelt down and slowly ran a hand over the belly of a pregnant heifer, evaluating. "What about you, Beth?"

"What about me?"

Dan stood straight and narrowed his eyes. "What's your story?"

"I don't have a story."

"I doubt that. Everyone has a story." He looked her up and down, but her face remained impassive. "I will say that you're nothing like I expected.

"What did you expect?"

"Oh, you know. City girl. A diva who's more concerned about her shoes than people."

"I like shoes." She released a small laugh. "A lot, actually."

He stared at her footgear. "Yeah, and those Mucks that Mom lent you look really good on you."

Beth examined the oversize rubber boots that came nearly up to her knees. A small smile lifted the corners of her mouth.

"So, where *are* you from?" Dan grabbed the pitchfork and headed to one of the only empty stalls.

"Here, there and everywhere."

"That sounds like someone avoiding a direct answer." He spread new hay into the space, then straightened, leaned on the fork and pinned her with his gaze.

"We traveled around a lot when I was a kid."

"We?"

"My mother and I."

"I got the impression you don't have a mother."

Beth turned away, looking at everything but him. "Everyone has a mother, Dan. Whether we like it or not."

"Why did you live with Ben?"

She took a deep breath, her back still to him. "My mother took off."

Dan grimaced, feeling the emotional sucker punch of her words. "I'm sorry. I—"

"It's not a big deal."

He dug the pitchfork into the hay with a vengeance. Life could be pretty unfair, and no matter how nonchalant Beth Rogers tried to sound, he knew that her mother leaving was a big deal. *A very big deal.*

A cow lowed loudly behind him.

"Uh-oh, I think we've got another delivery. You want to hold another tail?"

Beth turned. "Sure."

Dan led the mooing cow to the fresh stall and donned a clean glove to check the calf. "Joe is going to owe me big-time."

"Your brother is in Denver?"

"Yeah. Prosthesis fitting." He fastened the head gate around the heifer.

"Do you mind if I ask what happened?"

"He wrestled with a tractor and lost."

Beth gave a small gasp. "No."

"He was trying to make a repair, and the tractor ended up landing on him. By the time I got to him it was too late to save his arm. I rolled the tractor off and applied a tourniquet and got him to the Paradise Hospital. They sent him to Alamosa by Life Flight, but still couldn't save the arm. There was too much damage."

Elsie appeared at the barn door. She looked from Beth to Dan with speculation, a slight smile on her lips as usual. "Here you go."

Beth grabbed the oversize baby bottle and offered it to Dan as Elsie slipped back out of the barn.

"Want to feed the calf for me?" he asked Beth.

"Really?" Her brows rose. "All by myself?"

"Sure. I've got to stay here with this momma, but the baby needs that bottle. Tuck the calf firmly against you with an elbow and hold the bottle. That's all there is to it. They catch on pretty fast." Across the barn the baby cow stood next to the fence and stared woefully at them.

"Why are you feeding only one?" Beth asked.

"The momma is feeding the other one. She's a little confused, and doesn't realize this baby is hers as well."

"An abandoned baby." Beth sighed.

"Seems to be the theme around here," Dan murmured.

"What will happen to the one she doesn't acknowledge?"

"Time will tell. We may try to match her up with a cow that loses her calf. Bottom line is we'll try everything to make sure every calf survives."

Beth nodded.

"These cows are Joe's paycheck, and he gets paid only once a year, so every animal is valuable."

"He gets paid once a year?"

"When the cows go to market. It helps that he also grows and sells hay, but these cows are important." Dan slid on a glove and checked the heifer. "Breech," he muttered. With a shake of his head he yanked off the soiled glove. "Lord," he prayed. "I need this calf to change position. Soon, please. Amen."

"Do you always talk to God like that?"

"Like how?" Dan asked. He looked at Beth, but her face was obscured by a curtain of hair as she fed the calf.

"You know. Casually."

Dan frowned. "He's supposed to be our Father, right? So I talk to Him like He is one of the family."

"I've never heard of such a thing."

"Now you have," Dan said with a chuckle.

She repositioned her arm and checked the bottle. "We're done here," she announced.

"Great, thanks."

"What else can I do?"

"Take a break. I'm going to do another check on the pen. I'll be right back. Come and get me if this cow makes any noise."

"What exactly are you checking?"

"I'll evaluate the herd to see if any other calves have been born, and how they're doing. Then I'll be looking for signs of potential delivery problems. Heifers mostly. They're cows that have never given birth. We check the older cows as well to see how they're handling the weather."

"They stay out in the snow?"

"We can bring in the problems, but not all of them. They're cows, they'll survive. Besides, Joe has a small herd. Thankfully, this is a spring snow. It's cold, but it's not a bitter arctic blast." He grabbed his leather gloves. "There's always something to check around here. Feed. Fences. Cows. Chickens. Horses. Always something. I'm only grateful this is my brother's headache most of the time."

Dan opened the barn door and filled his wheelbarrow with feed cakes.

Across the barn, Beth Rogers sat in an old cane chair, hands in her lap and her head resting back against a wooden rail, sound asleep. She was going to have a stiff neck from that position. Dan debated waking her as he watched her peaceful breathing.

"I brought coffee." Behind him, his mother peeked around his shoulder.

He set down the wheelbarrow. "Thanks, Mom."

"She's sleeping," Elsie said.

"Yeah. The dogs were barking to be fed a while ago and she never even moved."

"Oh, goodness, poor thing. All tuckered out."

"She helped me pull another three calves, so she's earned the right to be tuckered out."

"Not too bad for a city girl," Elsie observed.

Dan smiled, his gaze lingering on Beth's profile. *No, not too bad at all.*

His mother glanced around the barn. "How do we stand?"

Dan yawned. "What day is it?"

She glanced at her watch. "You've been up for twenty-four hours. It's Monday, 5:00 a.m."

"Five o'clock. Mind telling me why you're up so early?"

"I never do sleep well when I know that you or your brother are out here working," she said.

"Prepare for another twenty-four to forty-eight hours of bad sleep, then," Dan said.

"I'm sorry for you, but Joe's sure going to be surprised. I guess this was a blessing. How would he handle pulling calves with one arm?"

"Oh, you know Joe," Dan said. "He would have

found a way. But, fortunately, he probably won't have to until he's got that prosthesis and has a chance to get used to it."

"Thank the good Lord you haven't had another medical run."

"I can agree with that. Have you seen a weather report?" Dan asked.

"The snow is expected to stop late Wednesday or into the early hours on Thursday. The airport says they anticipate all Thursday flights will be going out as usual."

Dan released a long, hard sigh. "That's good."

"Then why that look?" Elsie asked.

"Beth's got a flight out Thursday afternoon. She needs to be at the airport by Thursday noon at the latest."

"I guess we'll have to make sure we dig out fast enough to get her there on time, won't we?"

"That's what I said."

"All we can do is keep praying," his mother added.

Dan took the thermos. "Thanks for this." The hot beverage steamed as he poured it into the cup she had provided.

Elsie handed him two sandwiches from her pocket and nodded toward Beth. "Ham and egg on wheat with cheese. Should we wake her?"

"No, she's stubborn. If we wake her, she'll want to dive right back into helping. For some reason she feels she has to pull her weight. She said she won't go in until I do, so we may as well let her sleep."

"You explained that she's a guest?"

He looked at his mother as he accepted the sandwiches. "Tried that about six hours ago. She counters by telling me she is an uninvited guest."

Elsie frowned. "Hmm. There's more to Beth than she lets on. She reminds me of you."

"How's that?"

"You're both holding in more pain than you care to admit."

Dan's head jerked back at his mother's unnerving comment. She was closer to the truth than he was comfortable admitting. He opened his mouth and then thought better of responding.

"Maybe we can ask Ben about her," Elsie continued.

"Mom, no, she deserves her privacy."

"Oh, pooh, the girl is lost, anyone can see that."

"I wouldn't try that 'lost' line on Beth, either. I already did. Huge mistake. Trust me."

"You're a man."

"Yeah?" He unwrapped a sandwich and eagerly bit in. "Havarti?"

"Yes." Elsie smiled, obviously pleased that he noticed. "You know, Dan, men approach things differently than women."

"I don't know what you're getting at, but I'm thinking you just insulted me."

She chuckled. "I'm merely saying that sometimes a woman can open a door with the diplomacy that men lack."

"Yeah. You did insult me."

Elsie laughed again and swatted him. "Oh, hush. Never mind."

"Good sandwich."

"Thank you. I have cinnamon rolls baking, so I need to get back to the house." She glanced at Beth again. "You'd better wake her up soon and send her in."

"I'm headed in the house for a nap shortly. I'll wake her then."

Dan shoved the rest of the food into his mouth and picked up the wheelbarrow handles again. Once the feed cakes were distributed he checked on his orphaned calf. All was well in the barn. Rounds completed, he could risk a two-hour nap.

He stood over Beth and gently placed a hand on her shoulder.

Nothing.

"Beth." He tried calling her name a bit louder. "Beth."

She jumped and the chair began to tilt, threatening to crash sideways to the ground as her limbs flailed.

Squatting, Dan caught her in his arms and held her to him.

Beth slowly raised her lashes and met his eyes.

Noses nearly touching, they both froze. Seconds ticked by as her warm breath kissed his face. Dan swallowed. It took every last bit of resolve in him not to touch his lips to her soft inviting mouth.

Instead, he placed his hands on her waist. "You okay now?" he whispered.

She gave a wordless nod, her eyes round, as he released her.

"What happened?" she finally asked, her voice tremulous.

"I was, uh, trying to wake you up."

"What time is it?" Glancing around the barn, Beth winced and began to massage her neck.

"Five-thirty."

"That can't be right."

"'Fraid so."

Her eyes widened. *"In the morning?"*

Dan nodded.

"How long was I sleeping?"

"Only about two hours." He grabbed the thermos and motioned to the cup.

She shook her head. "No, thanks. Why did you let me sleep?"

"I didn't have the heart to wake you. You were exhausted."

"You must be, as well," she countered.

"I'm used to it. You aren't." Dan tossed her the other sandwich. "Ham and egg with Havarti. Fresh. My mom just made it."

"Thank you." Beth opened her mouth to say more and then closed it, without uttering a comeback. She stared at the wrapped food in her hand.

"I'm only trying to do my share," she said.

"No, you're trying to do your share and six other people's," Dan returned. "You like to keep the balance sheet in your favor."

To his surprise Beth gave him a grudging smile. "I never thought of it like that," she admitted. "Perhaps you're right."

He grinned, pleased for no good reason. Or maybe because they'd crossed an invisible milestone of trust. He didn't know why that pleased him, since she'd be gone soon, but it did.

Suddenly, the joy that had lightened his heart disappeared. *He really didn't want Beth Rogers to leave.*

Chapter Six

Beth sat down at the light oak, upright piano and stared out at the white landscape. She'd never seen so much snow before. The drifts were even creeping up to the window ledge.

She tossed her damp braid back and massaged her neck before glancing at the clock resting on piano. It was 11:00 a.m. She'd slept five hours, but Dan had barely napped before heading back out. A little longer to dry her hair and she'd go out to help him.

Her thoughts wandered to that moment when he'd woken her up in the barn. What was that, anyhow? Did he almost kiss her? Did she almost *want* him to kiss her?

"You have hair like me."

Startled, Beth turned to find Dan's daughter standing next to the piano. Today Amy had two tidy braids and wore sparkly pink shoes, and a pink tutu over her jeans and pink sweater. She had accessorized with several strands of plastic pearls that hung around her neck. Beth couldn't help but smile at the outfit.

"Yes. We both have braids today."

"GG fixed my hair." Amy smiled as she walked forward to examine Beth's braid.

"I see." Beth touched the tulle on Amy's tutu. "Are you a dancer?"

Amy nodded. "GG takes me to ballet and tap and jazz at Miss Cathy's. Sometimes Daddy takes me to Denver to see the real ballerinas dance."

"Your daddy must love you very much."

Amy nodded again, then paused, squinching up her nose. "Do you know my mother?"

"No. I'm sorry, but I don't."

The little girl's chin dropped to her chest and she released a pitiful sigh as she stared at the piano keys.

Beth understood that pain. She'd tortured herself with endless questions about her mother, until the day she'd finally found her, with a whole new family. Then all Beth had to do was get over the pain of realizing she was unloved. *And unwanted.*

But Amy Gallagher had a family. A family who obviously loved her very much. And Beth was an adult, with a full life and a successful career. So why was it that the sting of abandonment never went away?

Beth touched the smooth, well-worn ivory keys, allowing her index finger to rest on middle C. She pressed the key and the note sang into the room.

The little girl peeked at Beth from beneath her lashes. "Can you play?"

"I think so."

A shadow of a smile appeared as Amy slid onto the bench next to Beth. "This was my grandpa's piano. Daddy says Grandpa Gee played all the time."

Beth pressed middle C again. "Do you play?"

"No." Amy shook her head, offering another sad face.

Beth scooted down the bench, closer to the child. She picked up Amy's small hand and placed it on the keyboard an octave lower. Then she gently placed her finger on Amy's index finger and pressed. "This is low C."

"Low C," Amy repeated.

"Yes. Keep your hand there and when I nod my head, you press the key and low C will sing for us."

The little girl grinned.

Beth found herself slowly playing a song she vaguely remembered from long ago. Though she couldn't recall how she knew the piece, one-by-one the notes came back until she was actually moving through the entire melody, all the while nodding her head to indicate when it was Amy's turn. The short song concluded and Beth stopped, resting her hands in her lap in surprise.

Amy laughed, surprised as well. Her gray eyes sparkled with delight. "I played piano."

"Yes, you did."

"Play some more, please."

"Let's look in the bench and see if there's any music in there."

"Music in the bench?" Amy hopped off.

Nearly as excited as the little girl, Beth lifted the lid of the wooden seat. Inside were dozens of old sheets of music and several choir songbooks. Beth grabbed a stack of the sheets and sorted through them until she found one that was familiar.

Opening the pages, she placed the booklet neatly on the piano's music rack. She hesitated, then put her hands on the keyboard and began to read the music and play.

"'The love of Jesus fills my heart with endless joy and gladness.'" Elsie's clear voice filled the air as she entered the room, a towel on her shoulder. "'Fills my heart with endless joy and *gla-ad-ness*.'"

Beth finished playing the hymn as Elsie sang.

"GG, you know this song?"

"Of course."

Beth held back a laugh at Elsie's navy sweatshirt embellished with today's quote, Free Contradictions.

"You play nicely, dear," Elsie said.

"Thank you. I haven't played in years." Beth closed the music. "I hope you don't mind that I pulled these out."

"Oh, no, of course not. No one in this house plays anymore."

"Maybe Dr. Beth can teach me how to play, GG."

"Hmm, I don't know." Elsie looked to Beth and winked. "You'd have to be an awfully good girl. And you'd have to ask Dr. Beth."

When Beth turned to meet Amy's expectant face, she paused, arrested by exactly how much the little girl resembled her father. The eyes were identical, as was her nose and full contagious smile. A mini Dan with braids.

"You know, I'm only here for a few days," Beth said.

"That's okay. If you can teach me a little bit, then I can teach my dolls."

"I can do that."

"What do you say, Amy?" Elsie asked.

"Oh, thank you. Thank you." Amy launched herself at Beth, wrapping her arms around her waist and burying her head against her side in a bear hug.

"Ah!" Beth was taken by surprise, flushed with pleasure and nearly speechless. "You're welcome." She placed a hand on Amy's back and awkwardly patted her.

Amy straightened and stared intently at Beth for a moment. "And will you come to my special program, too? You can sit up in the front of the 'torium with Daddy and GG."

Beth looked to Elsie.

"There's a spring program. Amy's class is in it. Friday night."

"Oh, Amy, I'll be gone Friday night." Regret weighted upon Beth.

"You said a couple of days," Amy sniffed.

"Yes, but a couple doesn't last until Friday. I'll be leaving on Thursday. I'm so sorry." And she was, Beth realized. Very sorry.

Amy's full bottom lip quivered.

"Come on now," Elsie said to her granddaughter. "Time for you to clean up the playroom. We're supposed to make cookies today, aren't we?"

With a begrudging nod Amy dragged her feet slowly toward the door.

"Maybe Dr. Beth would like to help us make cookies." Amy stopped and looked up, her expression now hopeful.

"From scratch?" Beth asked.

"Is there any other way?" Elsie asked.

"I've never made cookies from scratch before," Beth admitted.

Elsie's eyes widened. "Oh, my, my. Then Amy and I will have to teach you how. Right, Amy?"

Amy's mouth curved into a smile.

"What kind of cookies shall we make with Dr. Beth?"

"Snickerdoodles!" Amy said.

"Then snickerdoodles it is. Hurry and put your toys away, first."

Amy clapped her hands and skipped down the hall.

"Whew, that was close. Glad we turned things

around." Elsie sighed. "Most of the time she's fine, but every now and again she gets a little needy. Little girls sometimes just want their momma, period." She met Beth's gaze. "What kind of mother abandons her child, do you suppose?"

Beth licked her lips and swallowed, suddenly feeling queasy. "I, um, good question."

"I suppose we should just be thankful that she gave Dan full custody."

"He's a good father," Beth murmured.

"Yes. The trouble is, Dan's so afraid of making a mistake again that he guards his heart and Amy like a momma bear."

"Don't you think that's natural?"

"Perhaps. But I can tell you this, there are half a dozen women in Paradise who would be happy to step in and remedy the situation. Dan won't have any part of it, however."

"It?" Beth asked, though she knew she shouldn't. Talking about Dan behind his back made her very uncomfortable.

"Oh, you know. Matchmaking. He claims that what happened with Amy's mother is the past, but in my opinion, he sure doesn't seem to be moving on." Elsie shrugged and then gave a little chuckle. "Of course, I have an opinion on everything."

Beth stood and replaced the sheet music inside the bench, carefully closing the lid.

"Are you and Dr. Ben close?" Elsie asked.

"Hmm?" Beth looked at her, unsure how to answer the question. "Close? I don't really know."

"You weren't at the wedding."

"I was under contract in Los Angeles. I couldn't get away."

"Family is important," Dan's mother observed.

Beth nodded, not sure how to respond. Such talk was always awkward.

Yes, she knew family was very important. Then again, she'd done fine—better than fine—without one, hadn't she?

"Now I'm curious. How is it you lived with Ben's family and never made cookies?" Elsie asked.

"I only lived with them for my senior year of high school, and, well, let's just say that it really wasn't my finest hour."

"Well, dear, I can tell you after raising four children, the teenage years aren't anyone's finest hour." Elsie paused and rubbed her sternum.

"Are you feeling all right, Mrs. Gallagher?"

"A little heartburn. I knew I shouldn't have added that red pepper to my soup." She smiled. "No worries. I'll have some milk and be fine."

The front door opened and Dan's booted feet could be heard coming down the hallway. Both women turned to look as he appeared.

"What?" he asked, his gaze taking in both of them.

"Nothing. Beth and I were merely chatting."

Dan narrowed his eyes at his mother and shook his head.

"You look exhausted. Is everything all right?" Elsie asked.

"Sure, I'm just knee-deep in fun."

"Do you want me to call Joe? Maybe he'll have suggestions."

"Yeah, he'll suggest I man up." Dan laughed. "Not a thing that Joe can do long-distance. Besides, I can handle knee-deep. When I get waist-deep, then I'll consider calling my big brother so he can give me a dose of patronization."

Elsie looked at Beth. "Brotherly competition. They've been like this all their lives." She turned back to him. "What's the plan?"

"Plan? I'm putting out fires. No time for a plan. I've got another breech waiting on me and a nervous heifer refusing to come into the barn."

"Breech? Is birth imminent?" Elsie asked.

"I have some time. I want to get the orphaned calf fed, and then I'm thinking we're due for a nice lull."

"I'll help," Beth said.

The tension in Dan's jaw eased. "That would be great. Same procedure as before. If you want to take over the next two feedings, well, that sure would be a big help."

"Absolutely," Beth said.

"Don't let her overwork herself this time, Dan."

"Who, me? I think Dr. Rogers likes being overworked."

Dan smiled, looking all the more attractive, despite his red eyes and stubble. This was a smile that was just for her, and it set off a funny tingle inside Beth, leaving her momentarily speechless.

Dan Gallagher thought he knew her, and that was worrisome. Yes, she liked to work, but she liked being needed even more. Dan needed her today. The key was to know when she wasn't needed anymore and to move on before she was left behind.

A thick cookbook, stuffed with scraps of paper, lay open on the kitchen table when Beth walked into the room. Amy knelt on a chair, her chin resting on her hands and her corduroy-clad bottom in the air as she waited patiently for the baking to begin.

"Where's your grandmother?" Beth asked.

Amy sighed. "An important phone call from the ladies zillery."

"The what?"

"The Paradise Ladies Auxiliary," Elsie said as she walked into the kitchen. "I'm sorry, Beth, but it actually *is* important. They're on hold. Do you mind?"

"Oh, no problem. I'll come back."

"No need. You can start without me."

"But I've never…"

Elsie waved a hand. "The recipe is right there.

Measure out the ingredients. Amy can show you where everything is. By then I'll be done. If I can get Bitsy Harmony to stop talking, that is."

When Elsie left the room, Beth turned to Amy. "I am confident we can do this."

"What does *confident* mean?"

"It means that if I can insert a triple lumen subclavian catheter in the carotid artery of a combative patient, the first time, then surely I can make snickerdoodles."

Beth read through the ingredients and looked up at Amy. "Measuring cup?"

Amy pointed to a cupboard.

Beth pulled out a large, five-cup glass measuring bowl with a spout. "Measuring spoons? Spatula?"

Her assistant hopped off the chair and pulled open a drawer. "Here."

"You're very good at this."

"GG showed me how to bake."

"Do you know what cream of tartar is?"

"No." Amy shook her head.

"Neither do I, but I hope we can find it in the refrigerator." She pulled open the door of the large side-by-side stainless steel fridge and examined containers of cream, tartar sauce, yogurt and milk. "No cream of tartar." She shut the door. "Let's do the flour and sugar. That's easy."

Amy raced to another cupboard and tugged open the double doors.

"Thank you." Beth took out a canister of flour and another of sugar. Then she looked through the spices. "Hey, cream of tartar. Who knew?" She grabbed the vanilla, salt and other seasonings and placed them on the table.

"Can I help?" Amy asked, as she resumed her position on the chair.

"Yes. You are my official mixer." Beth whirled around. "First we'll need some bowls."

"Way up there." Amy pointed to a shelf above the spice cupboard.

Beth chose two large pottery bowls.

"Three cups of flour." She eyed the bag of flour and the measuring cup. "I'll pour the flour into the cup and you pour it into the bowl."

"Okay."

Beth filled the container to the three-cup line, gently tapping to be sure she had exactly three cups full. "Your turn. It's heavy. Think you handle that?"

"Yes." Amy wrapped her little hands around the measuring cup and turned it upside down.

"Oh, oh, careful." Beth moved the bowl inches to the right. "Good to get it in and not miss."

And the flour did land in the bowl, with a soft thud, exploding into a cloud of dust.

Tiny prickles raced up Beth's arms.

Uh-oh. Maybe dumping wasn't a good idea.

Amy sneezed and more billows of flour clouded into the air, landing on both of them and dusting their faces, the table, chair, nearby countertops and even the floor with white.

Beth looked at Amy. There was even flour on her long eyelashes.

"Oh, no," Beth whispered, eyes wide with panic. "No. No."

"How are the bakers doing?" Dan stepped into the kitchen and stopped. He removed his hat and looked from Amy to Beth. His eyes popped and his mouth remained open, forming a perfect O.

And then he snorted a laugh. That was followed by huge choking laughter. Dan bent over and kept laughing as he held his hat in his hand.

Giggles slipped from Amy's mouth when she realized she wasn't in trouble.

"This isn't funny," Beth told him.

"You aren't standing where I am," he said.

"Your mother is going to have a fit. *Please.* Help me clean this up."

"Yes, ma'am." He straightened and wiped his eyes. "Spray cleaner is in the hall closet," he said, clearing his throat. "I'll get the broom. Amy, go wash that flour off your hands and face."

She bobbed her head, her eyes round as she turned and raced from the kitchen. "Yes, Daddy."

"Look at this place," Beth moaned as she sprayed down the table.

"Aw, it's just a little flour."

"Yes. It's just a little flour, but it's *everywhere.*"

"Not everywhere."

"Dan. It's everywhere."

"I think you should focus on the important thing here."

She paused midwipe and turned to look at him. "Excuse me?"

"You're making memories."

Beth released a sound between a squeak and a moan. "What kind of memories are these?" she asked, assessing the mess.

Dan stopped sweeping. "What kind of cookies are you making?"

"Snickerdoodles."

"Well, from now on every time Amy and I hear the word *snickerdoodles* we'll think of you." He snorted and burst out laughing yet again.

"Dan!" Beth shook her head, helpless to stop his laughter. "This isn't funny."

"Yeah. Actually, it is."

She groaned in frustration and began to race around the kitchen, spraying the appliances and the cupboards with a vengeance. When she ran a hand along the counter, there were still traces of flour on her palm. "I'm a doctor and I can't even make cookies without messing up," she muttered.

"Don't be so hard on yourself." Dan opened a cupboard door and dumped the contents of the dustpan in the trash. "Look, now we're as good as new."

He set the broom against the counter. "Well, except for you," he added.

Beth grabbed a paper towel and swiped it across her face.

"You missed some." He chuckled.

"Could you get it for me?"

"Hey, relax. My mother isn't going to have a fit."

"Her beautiful kitchen is covered with flour."

"Hardly any left. We got it all."

"I wish."

"Look, Mom had four kids. Count 'em. Four. This is nothing. You should have seen the food fights that happened around this kitchen. Not pretty."

"Food fights?"

"Yep." He nodded and looked at Beth with a grimace.

"Now what?"

Dan clucked his tongue. "Oh, this is bad."

She sucked in a breath. "Really?"

"Kidding." Dan wet a dish towel in the sink. "Close your eyes." He gently wiped the bridge of her nose and her eyelids.

She stilled at his touch, admonishing herself a second later. Good grief, the man was only wiping flour from her face. Was she going to swoon, too?

"So, how are we doing?" Elsie asked.

Beth's eyes flew open as Dan's mother sailed into the kitchen and paused.

"Oh." Elsie's ever-knowing smile got wider. "Am I interrupting something?"

Beth whirled around. "No."

"GG, I got flour all over," Amy said from behind her grandmother.

Amy still had streaks of flour in her bangs and Elsie brushed at them with her fingers. Then she began to laugh. "So I see. Well, you can't make really good cookies without a little flour spilling, right?"

Amy nodded.

Dan nodded.

Beth tensed and stood very still.

"The important thing is we're having fun," Elsie finished.

"We are, GG."

"Dan, are you having fun?" Elsie asked with a little smile.

"Yes, ma'am," he answered, his lips twitching.

"Beth, are you having fun?"

"I, um, well…" Her gaze moved to each of the smiling Gallagher faces. Finally, she allowed the tension that held her rigid to fall away. Beth released a small smile. "Yes, Mrs. Gallagher. I am having fun."

Chapter Seven

Dan flipped on the kitchen light and discovered Beth seated at the kitchen table, a cookie halfway to her mouth and a mug in her other hand.

He nearly laughed out loud at the guilty expression on her face. Guilty? Of what? Looking adorable, maybe.

She was still in jeans and a sweater, though it was after midnight and the rest of the household was in bed and asleep.

"Good cookies, huh?"

Her lips twitched as she met his gaze, and she blushed, a soft pink coloring her cheeks. She quickly turned her attention back to the window.

"Okay to keep the light on?" Dan asked.

"Yes. Of course."

"Another busy day," he commented.

"It was fun," she said.

"Fun? Doc, you've got a very twisted idea of fun."

He glanced at his watch. "What is this? Barely Tuesday, and you've been working as hard as me since you arrived."

"Not nearly as hard as you, but I'm glad I could help."

"How's it looking out there?"

"White."

"Yeah, but I checked the weather report and the storm is moving through faster than originally forecast. We should be able to start digging out today. That means if the weather holds you'll be able to make your Thursday flight without any problems."

Beth's face lit up. "Oh, that's wonderful. Thank you."

"Don't thank me. That's what you call answered prayer." He added a couple tablespoons of cocoa mix to a mug filled with water, and placed it in the microwave. From where he stood, waiting for the microwave to beep, he could see Beth's reflection in the window.

She was smiling. A good thing. He liked making her happy, and he was going to hate to see her go. Beth Rogers had grown on him.

Dan pulled his mug from the microwave. "Mind if I join you?"

"Not at all."

"Insomnia?"

She nodded.

He reached for a large, blue glass canning jar

on top of the refrigerator. He shook it and the contents rattled.

"What's this?" she asked.

"Homeopathic insomnia treatment." Dan unscrewed the tin lid and handed her the jar. "Letter tiles. Grab seven."

Beth reached in and methodically selected seven tiles. "What's the object of this treatment?"

"It's kind of like the board game without the board."

"I'm not familiar with the board game."

Dan raised a brow. *Why was he not surprised?* "You make a word with your pieces. Each piece has a point designation written on the tile. The person with the most points wins the round and gets to pick their tiles first. Use a blank tile and your word score doubles. Play all seven tiles at once and your word score triples. Points are cumulative and we play to one hundred."

"That could take a while," she observed.

"Nah. Ten minutes max. No worries. I won't let you suffer...much."

Beth sputtered. "I'm very good with words."

"Weapon of choice, I imagine."

She shot him a glare.

"Next to lethal stares, of course."

She struggled not to laugh. The tightly wound doctor was starting to loosen up.

"So why is it *you're* up so late?" Beth asked. "More calf births?"

"No. Quiet at the moment, so I ran over and checked on Joe's house and mine."

"Everything okay?"

"My housekeeper clearly wasn't able to make it through the snow, because my place looks exactly like it did when I left."

"You have a housekeeper?"

"No. I don't," he deadpanned.

Beth paused and blinked. "Oh, that was a joke."

Dan shook his head and chuckled. "Yeah. I was testing you. You failed, but don't worry, I'll keep trying."

Her lips curved into a smile over the top of her mug.

"Cocoa?" he asked.

"Yes." She looked at him as though waiting for the other shoe to drop. "Why?"

"No big deal, just wondered why you don't have any homemade marshmallows in that mug."

"Homemade marshmallows? Is that a joke, too?"

Dan tipped his chair back and opened a cupboard. He slid his hand inside and pulled out a large plastic bag, which he tossed to Beth. "Here you go. Best marshmallows in the world. Man, you really lead a sheltered life. You've got to get out more."

"I'm beginning to think you're right," she murmured as she examined the bag and took out a large fluffy square.

"Note the date and time," Dan said.

"Good to know you aren't a told-you-so type of person." She dropped the marshmallow in her cup and then pushed her tiles forward on the table, her expression triumphant. "*D-E-R-M-A*. Eight points."

"Not bad," Dan said, revealing his own tiles. "*Q-U-I-R-K*."

"You're missing the *u*."

He unfolded his fingers. A blank tile lay in the middle of his palm. "Double word score for a blank. That's thirty-four big points."

Beth narrowed her eyes as he scooped up their tiles and put them in the jar. He shook it before removing his new set of seven game pieces and offering the jar to her.

They silently studied their tiles.

Dan reached across the table and took a snickerdoodle from the foil-covered plate. "Pretty good cookies for a novice."

Beth looked up from rearranging the little wooden squares in front of her. "Who told you it was my first time making cookies?"

"Got it straight from the Gallagher 24/7 information hotline."

"You were talking about me?"

"No. I draw the line at gossip. But around here, listening is unavoidable. Collateral damage."

"You know, I have made cookies before. Lots of them." She moved her tiles around.

"Oh? Glad to hear that. What's your specialty?"

"Peanut butter. Chocolate chip. Sugar. Whatever's on sale. You know, the kind where you buy the dough and cut off a piece with a knife and then bake it."

"Are you talking about those refrigerator tube things?"

"Yes. They're perfectly acceptable."

Dan chuckled. "They're cheating."

"Not in my world they aren't."

He shook his head. "You're kinda hard to figure, aren't you?"

"Me?"

"Yeah. How is it you grew up without baking cookies from scratch?"

"My own fault, really. I was a relatively antisocial kid."

"Not *you!*"

She offered him a short, embarrassed laugh and then cleared her throat. "I spent a lot of time in foster care trying hard not to fit in."

"Open mouth, insert foot. I'm sorry, Beth. I had no idea." *And I'm an insensitive idiot.*

"As I said, my own fault," she returned. "I certainly never made it easy on myself."

"How did you end up in foster care?"

"Ben and his family traveled a lot, doing missionary work, so they hadn't been in contact with my mother for a long time. She didn't want contact. Ben's father is her half brother."

"I'm confused." Dan cocked his head in question.

"When my mother left me, they had no idea. There was no way for me to contact them, either."

"She just took off and didn't look back?"

"Pretty much. We were on another of our many road trips. She dropped me off at a café, next to a truck stop in a little town on the Colorado-Kansas border. Holly, Colorado." She met his gaze. "Did you know that Holly is the lowest-elevation town in all of Colorado?"

"Um, no." Dan swallowed hard. "What about your father?" he asked, still trying to digest the bomb Beth had shared so casually.

She shrugged. "No idea."

"How old were you when she, ah, she left you?"

"Twelve."

He released a ragged breath.

"There's no need to get all worked up about it. It was a long time ago," Beth commented, once again switching her tiles around.

He gripped his mug. "I am all worked up about it. Have you seen your mother since?"

"I tracked her down a few years ago. She's got her life together. New family and everything."

"Did you talk to her?"

"Why?" Beth shrugged. "What would be the

point? I've closed that door. I understand that she did what she felt she had to do. Considering the circumstances, I got off easy."

Easy? Dan was speechless at her words.

Beth studied her tiles for a long time, before finally raising her head. "I'm ready."

"Okay. What've you got?"

"F-U-N."

"That's appropriate," he said drily. "How many points?"

"Six." She sighed. "I'm not crazy about this game."

"You like to win."

"Absolutely."

"You can always concede."

"Don't be ridiculous. I'm not a quitter." She glanced over at his tiles. "What do you have there?"

"Pulseox." Dan narrowed his eyes, mentally calculating the score. "Sixteen points, times the triple word is forty-eight. Plus the thirty-four. So that gives me eighty-two." He grinned and glanced at his watch. "What did I tell you? Ten minutes and—"

Beth whipped up a hand into the air, in a "talk to the palm" move. "No. No. No. *Pulseox* is not one word. Not only that, it's an abbreviation."

"Sure it's a word."

"Are you serious?"

Dan bit his cheek, trying to stave off a belly laugh.

Her blue eyes were fired up. *"That is not a word!"* she repeated.

"Everything okay in here?" Elsie walked into the room. She glanced from Dan to Beth and frowned. "Are you two fighting?"

"Professional disagreement. Did we wake you?" Dan asked.

"No, I was already awake. I thought I'd better tell you that when I peeked outside I'm pretty sure I saw a cow in the road."

Dan stood, sloshing his cup of cocoa. "A cow in the road!"

"The drifts have obscured the fence line, so I could be wrong, but I think a section of fencing has blown over."

He groaned.

Beth looked up at him. "You have to go outside for one cow?"

"If there's one, there's more that got out. Trust me." He shook his head. "And here's the irony. We'll get them all in tonight, and tomorrow I've got to move them all to the other pen so I can clean this one out."

"Do you want help?" Beth asked, as he headed for the door.

Dan looked at her. He didn't need help, but how could he resist, especially knowing she would be gone soon? "Sure," he said. "I'll get the four-wheeler." He turned and pinned her with a gaze. "Don't touch my tiles."

Beth only shook her head as she stood to find her coat.

"Wave my arms and yell?" Standing outside the feeding pen fence in thick, wet snow, Beth looked at him as though he was absolutely nuts. "What's the object of this exercise?"

Dan chuckled at the expression on her face. "A little analytical, aren't you?"

She shot him one of her intellectually superior glares that he was coming to recognize meant she was out of her depth and didn't like it one bit. "I don't think it's analytical at all. I simply want to understand the rationale behind jumping up and down and yelling at your bovine friends."

Dan stuck a pair of wire cutters into his back pocket. "Look, it's really simple. Cows are not the brightest animal God created," he said. "You can't tell them to come, so we have to scare them into turning around."

"Seriously, modern technology hasn't come up with a better plan than this?"

"When it comes to ranching, sometimes the old traditions are the simplest. Besides, the dogs will help you."

She glanced skeptically at the two black-and-white border collies that ran around in circles at her feet. "I still feel ridiculous," she muttered.

"No one other than me will ever know, and the cows aren't going to tell." He pounded the last stake in the fence and tugged on the barbed wire. "Okay, all fixed. You wave at them I'll stay inside the fence so none of them slip out."

"Why can't I stand inside the fence?"

"Because you don't know how to handle cows if they decide to get ugly, that's why."

"Oh." Her head jerked back a little at the implication. A moment later she began to enthusiastically wave her arms and call loudly, "Let's go cows. Go-o-o!"

"That's it. Keep moving toward the pen."

"Cowy. Cowy. Cowy. Rawhide."

Dan snorted.

"Woot. Woot. Woot." Beth sliced her arms up and down in the air like a madwoman. But the technique worked and the recalcitrant cows slowly trudged through the snow in the direction of the pen.

Dan patted the hind side of the animals as they moved through the gate, the dogs barking alongside and nipping at their heels. "Way to go, Rowdy," he called to Beth.

"Mo-o-ove, cow. Move!"

"You can stop now. They're all in."

She looked around. "So they are."

"You did a great job."

"Seriously?"

"Yeah." He fastened the gate. "Seriously."

"Thank you," she said with a little smile.

"We're going to have to haul some hay out here before we go in."

"Hay? Um, how are we going to do that?"

"Don't look so nervous. It's lots easier than screaming at cows in the middle of the night."

"That's reassuring."

"You wait right here. I'll be back with the flat-bed and a pitchfork. All you'll need to do is open the gate so I can move the truck in, and then close it behind me so those wily cows don't escape again. I'll do the rest.

He whistled and the dogs followed him. "Come on, guys, time for you to get back to the barn for the night."

Minutes later, Dan backed the ranch truck into the pen and got out.

"Now what?" Beth asked.

He jumped onto the flatbed. "Roll the hay off."

"I can help with that."

"Okay. Sure." Dan reached out a hand and Beth took it. He hauled her up on the truck in a swift movement. She stood next to him, her nose red and a grin on her face.

"Why are you smiling?" he asked.

"This is fun."

"Do you have fun being a doctor?"

She shrugged. "It's what I do."

"But is it fun?"

"Apples and oranges. It's like you being a pharmacist and working the rescue team. You do one and love the other."

"Are you telling me you love working on the ranch?"

"Maybe it's a novelty, Dan, but I really do like being outside and feeling a part of things." Looking at him from beneath her lashes, she said softly, "Maybe you're the one who's being a little analytical this time."

Dan grinned. "Touché, Doc."

And he was still smiling as he pulled his leather gloves from his pockets and slipped them on. He positioned his hands on the bale strings and shoved the hay off the truck. Reluctant to move, the cows lowed in protest and finally ambled out of the way when the hay hit the ground with a loud whooshing thud. Together Dan and Beth rolled two more bales into the pen.

"That's it?" she asked as she brushed the fine layer of hay dust from her clothes.

Jumping from the truck to the ground, Dan grabbed a pitchfork. "I'll spread it out and we're done."

Minutes later he leaned on the pitchfork, catching his breath. "What are you looking at?" he asked Beth.

She turned around from where she'd been lean-ing against the hood of the cab and staring out at the pasture. "It's like a picture postcard."

Dan climbed up onto the flatbed and stood next to her. She was right. The tall conifers were dark shadows stretching their fingers into the moonlit night. In front of them, the untouched blanket of snow spread for miles. The surface sparkled in the glow of the moon like thousands of scattered dia-mond chips.

"Perfect for snow angels, huh?"

Beth turned to face him. "Snow angels?"

"Don't tell me you never made a snow angel, either?"

"Another hole in my life's repertoire." She sighed.

"We can patch that hole pretty quick. Let move the truck first."

Beth's eyes brightened. "Really? Right now?"

"Sure."

Dan held out a hand and helped her down from the flatbed, then pulled the truck out of the pen and parked it along the ranch road. He couldn't help smiling as he waded through the snow, back to where Beth waited. It seemed that he smiled an awful lot when she was around. "Pen locked up?" he asked.

She gave an enthusiastic nod.

"Okay, come on and I'll teach you the basics of

the classic snow angel." He stepped toward her and pulled up her collar.

"You're going to need to put your scarf on your head so your hair doesn't get all frozen with snow."

She quickly covered her head with the scarf and tucked in the ends.

"Now watch very carefully. This is very complicated. But you're a doctor, so there's no reason you can't do this."

She narrowed her eyes. "You're messing with me again, aren't you?"

Dan held up a finger. "Wait for it." He fell backward onto the ground, the thick snow providing a soft cushion.

"What are you *doing?*"

"Just watch." He slid his arms up and down. "Arms first. That makes the angel wings."

Beth's shoulders shook as she silently laughed, a mittened hand covering her mouth. Her blue eyes bubbled over with mirth.

"Any questions on the technique?"

"I…I don't know where to begin. It's difficult, but I think I might be able to do that."

"That's the spirit. Now for the legs. Ready?"

This time she giggled. *Dr. Elizabeth Rogers giggled.*

Ben moved his legs awkwardly back and forth,

pushing snow aside. "The key is to think jumping jacks."

"Got it." She shook her head. "What a time to be without my camera. We could have videotaped this and I'm sure it would have gone viral."

"Cowboys don't go viral," he said.

Beth laughed.

"Now the tricky part is getting up."

"Want help?'

"No. No. Stay where you are or it will mess with the silhouette." Dan sat up and then moved to his knees. Grunting, he hauled himself to a standing position. "Gets a little harder to get up, every year."

He stepped out of the angel and turned to assess his creation. "Not bad."

"It's beautiful." Her voice was laced with awe, the words heartfelt.

"Are you ready to try?"

"Yes."

Dan stuck out a hand, offering her the pasture as her canvas. "After you."

Beth dropped onto the ground and moved her legs and arms at the same time. She sat up and jumped lithely to a standing position.

"That was the fastest snow angel I've ever seen." Dan clapped his gloved hands together.

She gave an exaggerated bow before turning to look at the snow behind her. "Oh, that is absolutely perfect."

"Nice job. Turn around and I'll dust you off."

"I've got it." She stomped her feet and shook her head. "That was so much fun."

"Do you want to do it again?" he asked.

Her lips parted and she let out a little gasp of surprise. "Can we?"

"Well, yeah."

Beth nodded, excitement thrumming in her eyes. Her face was rosy from the cold and her teeth chattered, but she kept right on smiling, like a kid.

Over and over again they fell backward, down on the wet snow to create an angel, and then got up and made another one. Beth's laughter rang out as she tore across the pasture.

Finally she stood, bent over, panting and laughing. "That was the best."

"You're obviously way younger than me. I think I made only half as many as you, didn't I?"

"Not telling."

"Ready to go in?" he asked.

"Yes. I'm wet and c-c-cold." She looked behind her once more at the field of angels. "But this was so worth it." Dan grinned at her expression.

They began walking toward the truck. Beth stumbled and Dan slipped an arm around her waist to catch her.

"Thank you," she said, her voice breathless.

"You've got hay in your hair."

"Do I?"

Dan reached over and pulled the stick out. Her gaze met his and they both stopped, their movements slowing down.

He leaned toward her.

She leaned toward him.

"This isn't a good idea," he murmured.

"Probably not," she whispered, her warm breath making little condensation clouds before caressing his face.

And then he kissed her. His hand reached up to gently cup the back of her head, and his cold mouth met her cool lips. It was a slow, leisurely kiss, yet his heart pounded with the rightness of the woman in his arms.

Finally, Dan released her, and by then both their lips were warm.

Beth sighed and her lashes fluttered open. "Dan, I…"

Though he liked the sound of his name on her lips, he stilled her words with a finger on her mouth. "No analyzing tonight."

She returned a shy nod.

"Tomorrow, maybe. But I'm too tired tonight. Okay?"

"Okay," she murmured.

"Let's get some rest and forget about everything, especially cows, for a couple of hours at least."

She smiled.

Yeah, if only for a couple of hours, he wanted—no, he needed—to pretend that this moment, this time with Beth, was something he could keep.

Chapter Eight

Beth sat at the window of the guest bedroom looking out at the clear night sky while she slowly ran a comb through wet strands of hair. She could see the barn in the distance and the dark outline of the cows in the feeding pen. If there was a slice more of bright moonlight she'd be able to see the pasture and the dozens of snow angels she and Dan had created merely an hour or so ago.

She was exhausted, yet despite how physically tired she was, she still couldn't sleep. Her mind refused to slow down. Thoughts crowded in. Yes, she had a lot on her mind.

Why did that always seem to be her mantra? *A lot on her mind?*

Probably because she had spent her entire life trying to stay one step ahead of everyone. Because she was a fraud, an imposter who was terrified that if people really got to know her, they would reject her.

Except the Rogerses didn't, the voice of reason whispered.

Ben's parents were lovely people, but they had to like her, didn't they? She'd been thrust upon them by social services. They didn't have a choice. She was their niece, so they were forced to accept the abandoned girl. That was how the rationalization had always started. Except this time it was different.

The Gallaghers had welcomed her into their home like, well, like family. Beth was at a loss to understand how the relationship that had developed with this family was forged so easily and in such a short time, but she couldn't deny how attached she felt to Elsie and Amy.

Then there was Dan.

Beth slowly touched her lips with her fingers. *That kiss.* She hadn't been kissed in a long time and never by anyone who mattered.

Dan Gallagher mattered.

She didn't know why, but he did. He made her feel normal. Like she didn't have to try. Didn't have to have her fences in place. She could be herself and that was more than good enough.

Somehow Dan had slipped beneath her wall of defense to get closer than anyone ever had. What was she going to do? Because eventually Dan would realize that she wasn't the kind of woman he was looking for. The kind of woman to be his wife, or Amy's mother.

The only thing she could do effortlessly was be a doctor. Medicine was her life, her default.

Beth released a sigh. Mostly she couldn't sleep because she had lied to Dan. That weighed heavily on her heart. Technically, it wasn't a lie. It was an omission. Because she *had* approached her mother. Beth had met her mom for coffee, like two old friends.

Lidia. Lidia Smith or Jones. *Whatever.* Lidia had said Beth was a mistake, one in a long line of mistakes. But that was the past, the woman who had once been her mother announced, right before she'd begged Beth not to tell her husband.

No tender reunion and certainly no apology for leaving Beth behind like an unwanted pet. She'd barely been able to make eye contact, and clearly wanted to be rid of Beth as soon as possible.

So Beth had walked away, shame burning her cheeks. Her heart pierced yet again.

She closed her eyes now and swallowed the memory of that painful afternoon. Putting the comb away, she reached for her computer tablet on the oak bureau, intending to review her five-year plan. There was always comfort in reviewing that file. The graph. The bullet points. She could find peace in each detailed step and substep. She was almost there.

New York was within her grasp. Job security in a prestigious practice. Locked into a nice benefit package. A rent-controlled condo after six weeks. A place to finally call home and put down roots.

But instead of the tablet, her hand found the Bible. She tugged the leather-bound book to the bed and looked at it with doubt. What could this book possibly offer that her five-year plan couldn't?

A scarlet cord marked a page where someone had last been reading. Beth carefully turned back the pages until the book lay open.

The date scribbled in the margin was six years ago.

When Elsie's husband had died. The same time Dan had come back to Paradise with his baby girl.

Beth whispered the underlined verse aloud. "John 3:16 'For God so loved the world, that He gave his only Son, that whoever believes in Him should not perish but have eternal life.'"

Though Beth was very still, her heart raced.

God. Her heavenly Father.

It was as though He was calling her name. Calling her to Him.

This time Beth didn't hesitate to answer and welcome the Lord into her heart.

The knock at her bedroom door had Beth scrambling with the covers and nearly falling out of bed. The Bible was still open on the quilt next to her.

"Coming." She stumbled into her jeans and threw

the same sweater she'd been wearing for two days over her sleep shirt before pulling open the door.

It was Elsie. Dan's mother sported a bright red sweatshirt that said Don't Make Me Use My Mom Voice.

"Did I oversleep?" Beth ran a hand through her hair. She'd fallen asleep with a wet head. No doubt her hair was now bent, spindled and folded every which way.

"No. No. It's only 6:00 a.m.," Elsie said.

"Is everything okay?"

"I'm not feeling quite right, dear, and I wondered if, well, I thought that maybe you could check me out. I don't want to worry Dan. He has enough going on."

Beth really looked at Elsie Gallagher. Her color was ashen and anxiety pulled at the corner of lips. "Come on in, Mrs. Gallagher."

"Oh, please, not Mrs. Gallagher. I feel like we know each other too well for that. I'm Elsie to my friends. And you are definitely a friend."

Beth smiled, realizing that she felt exactly the same way.

"Why don't you sit, Elsie?"

"Don't you love this chair?" Elsie asked as she lowered herself to the peach Parsons chair. "I covered it myself, you know."

"It is lovely," Beth agreed.

Elsie's gaze moved to the bed. "You've been reading the Bible? It's an extra one. You can take it with you if you'd like."

"I…um, yes. Thank you. So, Elsie, can you describe your symptoms?"

"I believe it began last night. I felt off. Remember? I had a touch of heartburn."

Beth nodded, fighting a growing niggle of concern.

"I was lying down, trying to sleep, and I don't know.… There was a bit of pressure and burning in my chest and my heart was thumping much too fast. I almost felt… Well, like it was a little hard to breathe, as well. So I got up and sat in my chair for a while, praying, but I couldn't sleep. I was almost afraid to close my eyes." She met Beth's gaze. "This sounds silly, doesn't it?"

"No, Elsie, it isn't silly at all. It's very important that you are in touch with what you're feeling. If you think of anything else I want you to tell me."

Elsie gave a small nod. Her eyes were narrow with worry and the usual carefree laughter was nowhere to be found this morning. Instead she clasped and unclasped her hands in her lap.

"Are you in pain?"

"No. Not now, but last night I hurt. Though I wouldn't call it pain exactly. Maybe an ache."

"How's your breathing? Are you experiencing any light-headedness or shortness of breath right now?" Beth asked.

"Maybe a tiny bit, but goodness, I did run down the stairs." Elsie shrugged. "I almost feel like a fraud for bothering you."

"You were very wise to wake me up."

"You don't think it's anything serious, do you?" She pinned Beth with her gaze.

Practiced at avoiding a direct answer and keeping her patients calm, Beth answered slowly, "I'm a doctor and Dan is a skilled paramedic. You're in good hands."

"Yes. Yes. You're right. I hadn't thought of it that way."

"Do you mind if I take your pulse and listen to your heart?"

"You have a stethoscope with you?"

"I travel a lot, so I always carry mine in my purse." She pulled out her trusty black Littmann.

"That's handy."

Beth smiled at Elsie. "It is today." She took her pulse and listened to her heart. *Strong and regular.* "Can you lean forward and take a deep breath and hold? Now release your breath." *No rubs noted. Lungs clear to auscultation.*

"Everything okay?"

"So far. Do you have any allergies, Elsie?"

"Not that I know of."

"Are you on any medications?"

"Something for cholesterol. It's in the cupboard over the sink."

Beth nodded. She pulled out her tablet computer from her purse and made notes. "Any medical conditions, besides the cholesterol? A history of heart problems? Diabetes, or anything else you might be seeing your doctor for?"

"No. Except that he keeps nagging me to lose a few pounds." Elsie tugged down her sweatshirt. "I think a few extra pounds help to keep a mature woman looking younger. Plumps out those wrinkles. What does he know?"

Beth nodded in agreement as she entered information on the tablet. "Do you have any baby aspirin in the house?"

"Yes. That's over the sink, as well. I keep all the medicine there, out of the reach of children, of course."

"Very good. I'll be right back, but please, don't get up. Sit back and relax. All right?"

"All right, dear. If you say so."

Beth grabbed Elsie's cholesterol med and the baby aspirin, along with a glass of water. "Only one," she told Elsie, when she returned. "Now, I'm going to need to wake up Dan."

"Is that really necessary? You know he's probably only slept a couple of hours, if that. And if we tell him I'm not feeling well then he'll call Joe, and Joe will call his sisters, and that will start the avalanche of phone calls. They'll insist they have to come down here."

"You're loved," Beth observed.

"Yes. Yes. That's true," Elsie said.

"It's imperative that we get you to the hospital in Paradise to be properly checked. *Soon.*" Beth patted her hand.

Elsie released a sigh of resignation. "All right, dear. I suppose you do know what's best."

"Which room is Dan's?"

"Upstairs, last door at the end of the hall."

While Beth worked diligently to keep Elsie calm, she herself was beginning to feel the stress, because her gut said Elsie had had a heart attack.

If it was a heart attack, the aspirin would help, and if not, it wouldn't hurt. The bottom line was that Elsie needed to get to the hospital fast.

Dan had said the snow was tapering off. They had Joe's big pickup, and Dan had a defibrillator and basic medical supplies, so they would be able to monitor Elsie's ECG on the way to the hospital.

What else was there to do? Beth flashed back to the Bible in her room.

Pray.

That single word filled her spirit and she stopped in the middle of the stairwell and sat down, her hands folded, the only way she'd ever known to pray.

"Dear Lord," she whispered. "I have to call on You again. Please give me the wisdom to help this family the way You know is best, and guide me as I treat Elsie. Amen."

Beth took a deep breath and stood, feeling at peace before she raced up the staircase and pounded on Dan's door.

When the door flew open, she nearly toppled over.

"Whoa."

Dan was already up and dressed. He steadied her with a hand on her arm.

"You're up," she said.

"Yeah. What happened to your hair?" he asked with a chuckle.

She patted down her hair again. "Uh, look…I, uh…"

He frowned. "Everything okay?"

"Your mother isn't well."

"What happened?" Dan's face paled and he gripped the doorknob, prepared to move.

Beth put a hand on his arm. "Stop," she said.

"What do you mean, stop?" Pain flashed across his face. "Is she okay?"

"She's stable. In my room. And if you want her to stay calm then *you* need to stay calm. I gave her a baby aspirin. Right now her heart rate is regular and she's a little short of breath. I'd say she's either had an ischemic attack or some pretty severe angina."

"What do you want to do?"

"Can you please get the portable oxygen and the

defibrillator, and I'll hook her up. Then I'd like to start an IV, so we have an open line in case we need one. I'll stay with her until you get the supplies."

"Do you want me to start the IV? I'm guessing it's been a while since you did that in the field."

"It's your mother. I think I should start one. And it hasn't been that long."

"Okay, but I'm here if you need me."

"Thanks. Go ahead and contact the Paradise Hospital. Let them know we're coming and ask them to be prepared for a cardiac incident. I'd feel better if Ben was there, as well."

Dan nodded. "We can take Joe's truck. I'll call the sheriff. If we get stuck in the snow, I want someone from the sheriff's department watching for us, and they've got a truck with a snowplow."

"Do you think we can make it into Paradise?"

"We'll find out." He reached out and put his hand on her shoulder, his gray eyes cloudy with emotion. "Thank you," he whispered. "It's not a coincidence that you were stranded with us, Beth. Thank you for stepping up when the family…" he cleared his throat "…when I needed you."

"You're welcome," she breathed.

Dan followed her downstairs to the guest room, where he knelt in front of his mother. "Mom, how're you feeling?"

"Not my best," Elsie admitted.

"You know that between God, me and Beth, we have you covered." He looked at Beth. "Right?"

"Yes. We're the A-team, Elsie."

She smiled. "I like your team."

"I'm going to get my defibrillator and then we can see what your heart is doing," he said as he stood up.

"What about Amy?" Elsie said.

"I'll wake her," Dan replied.

"I'm up." Amy rushed into the room, barefoot, her hair askew, but dressed in jeans and a sweatshirt. She launched herself at her grandmother. "Are you sick, GG?"

"Only a little," Elsie admitted.

"Then we need to pray, GG," Amy said, her face earnest.

Dan stood behind his daughter, his hands resting on her shoulders. "Amy is so right." He took his mother's hand and Beth's as Amy closed the circle. "Lord, we ask You to prepare the way as we drive into Paradise. Please keep us safe. And we ask You to hold my wonderful mother close to You and give us wisdom in this situation. Thank You. Amen."

"Why are we going to Paradise?" Amy asked.

"GG needs a checkup, so we all get to go for a ride. Come on," Dan said, holding out his hand for his daughter. "Let's grab a blanket and put some books in your backpack. You can sit in the front of the truck with me and be my navigator."

"I need socks, too, Daddy."

"And socks, too."

"Can Millie come?"

"No, Millie will stay home and watch the house for us," Dan said. "She's our watchdog, right?"

Amy nodded.

Dan returned minutes later with the defibrillator, the portable oxygen, his medical supply tackle box and a package containing a nasal cannula.

"I've got it," Beth said, reaching for the defibrillator first. "You can go ahead and make those calls."

He nodded gravely, hesitant to leave.

"We're good," Beth insisted, watching him leave. She stuck the three leads on Elsie and turned on the machine.

"What do those lines mean?" Elsie asked.

"They're indicators to tell us how your heart is pumping."

"Is it pumping okay?" she asked, her eyes on the dark screen.

"Everything looks good, but we'll keep you connected to the machine until we get to Paradise so we can keep an eye on things."

Beth tore the plastic off the nasal cannula and attached it to the oxygen tank. "Okay, let's get the tube around your neck and in place."

"Feels a little funny."

"It will smell a little funny at first, too, but then it will warm up. You'll get used to it and then you'll forget it's even there."

"You're the doctor." Elsie smiled. "I always wanted to say that."

Beth smiled back. "Okay, I'll need you to push up that sleeve on your arm. I'm going to start an IV."

"I liked you until you said that," Elsie returned. "I'm not going to watch."

"This will go quickly," Beth said, as she attached the tubing to the IV bag and placed it on the desk. "Any reactions to Betadine?"

Elsie shook her head.

Beth quickly applied the rubber tourniquet and found a nice plump vein in Elsie's left wrist. She pulled out a large bore IV catheter kit.

"If I do this nicely they won't have to start another one at the hospital," she said.

"I'm all for that."

Beth worked quickly, and soon the IV was hooked up.

"Can I look now?"

"Yes. All done. Let me see if Dan is ready."

Beth met him in the hall, right outside the guest room.

"We're set," he said, his voice low. "Here's Mom's coat. Oh, and Ben will meet us there. How's the ECG look?"

"Definitely some elevated ST segments," Beth said quietly.

Dan ran a hand over his face at her words. "It was a heart attack."

"Probably."

"She still hooked up?"

"Yes. I'll sit with her and monitor. Let's keep your tackle box in back of the truck with me."

"Okay. I'll get Amy in the truck and pull it around."

Beth walked back into the room. "Here's your coat, Dan is bringing the truck to the front door."

"What will they do at the hospital?" Elsie asked as she slipped her free arm into the sleeve of the coat Beth held for her, and draped the other side over her shoulder.

"They're going to want to do a lot of blood tests, and a full echocardiogram. Possibly a nuclear scan to check your heart, and some invasive tests."

"Invasive?"

"That's a fancy way of saying that they might have to actually go inside your body to check things out."

"But do they have to admit me?"

"Yes. Absolutely. For the tests and to monitor your heart."

"I can't stay in the hospital!" Elsie's voice became shrill with anxiety. "Who will take care of Amy and Dan? The ranch…" Her head dropped to her chest.

Beth knelt down next to Elsie and took her hand. "We have to do what's best for you," she said softly but firmly, meeting Elsie's worried gaze. "Your heart is talking to us and saying loud and clear that there is a problem. It isn't getting enough oxygen. This is serious and we have to listen to it. Time is very, very important. We have to get you to the hospital now."

"But—"

"Do you trust me, Elsie?"

"I do."

"Then know that I promise to help."

"You have to get to New York. That's more important."

"Elsie, you are my first priority. You take care of everyone else. Now it's time to take care of you."

"But your flight…"

"There will be other flights."

"But—"

"When I first got here," Beth interrupted, her voice calm and even, "do you remember what you told me? You said, 'He has a plan.'"

Elsie took a deep breath and slowly a smile curved her lips. "Yes, I remember. Funny how our words come back to haunt us."

Beth smiled at the admission. "So can we agree to put all of this in God's hands?" she asked.

"Yes. You're right. We'll do that." Elsie covered Beth's hands with her own. "Thank you, dear, for helping me to put it all in perspective."

Beth looked up and saw Dan standing in the doorway. His lips were thin and his jaw clamped tight. Something was wrong. *Very wrong.*

When his gaze connected with hers the expression was gone and the Dan she knew was back.

"Ready to go?" she asked him.

He nodded, giving away nothing.

"You want to carry the defibrillator and I'll carry the oxygen and the IV bag?" she asked.

Again, Dan nodded wordlessly.

Together, they eased Elsie into the backseat of the big truck, and Beth checked the tubing and wires.

"All set, Mom?" Dan asked as he closed his door and began to fasten his seat belt.

"Yes. Do you think we could stop at Patti Jo's Café for a pastry on the way?"

"No, Mom. Not today." Dan shook his head, his lips twitching.

"Fine." Elsie sighed. "You and Beth are a lot alike, you know. You're both no fun."

Chapter Nine

When Dan pulled up to the Paradise E.R., he saw Dr. Ben Rogers waiting inside the double-glass revolving doors. The hospital's circular drive had been plowed and the ground was wet and sprinkled with snow melt. Towering snowbanks hovered along the perimeter, a testament to the recent blizzard.

Sheriff Sam Lawson strode toward them from his patrol car in time to join Ben, who approached the truck with a wheelchair. Sam was a good guy and he made it his business to know everyone in Paradise, no matter how young or old. The sheriff stuck out a hand for a hearty handshake. "I'm relieved you made it in, Dan. How were the roads?"

"Not nearly as bad as they were on Saturday, that's for sure," he said.

"Glad to hear that. The Colorado Department of Transportation has promised to get them plowed all the way through Paradise by this afternoon."

"What's going on with your mother?" Ben asked in a low voice, after nodding to the sheriff.

"Her ECG indicates a possible heart attack," Dan murmured. "Apparently she had symptoms last night, but didn't tell us until this morning. Though her sinus rhythm has been stable, the ST segment is definitely elevated. Beth has her on two liters of oxygen and gave her a baby aspirin. IV is started." He shook his head. "The hard part was getting her here. She's already come up with a dozen reasons why she should be home."

"That's our Elsie," Sam said.

Dan pulled open the back passenger door and assisted Beth out first. She held the portable oxygen tank and the defibrillator in her hands.

"Mom, Dr. Rogers and Sheriff Lawson both came out to see you. You're a regular celebrity."

"Oh, I hate to keep Sam from his work, and, Ben, you need to get home to your babies. I'm only sixty-eight, not nearly old enough for this special treatment."

"Mrs. Gallagher, I wanted to be here. Besides, I heard all about those snickerdoodles you made. I thought there might be some in my future if I was real nice to you," Ben said.

Elsie's laughter rang out, the first laugh from her in hours.

Then she spotted the wheelchair.

"Really? Come on, boys. I imagine I could out-run all three of you. Do I really need this?"

"Protocol," Ben said with a chuckle.

"Oh, pooh."

Elsie held Dan's arm and slid from the truck's high seat until her feet touched the ground. She turned and settled into the wheelchair and shot Dan her best "I am the mother and I am very unhappy" look.

"Hey, Ben, thanks for being here," Beth said as she hooked the oxygen tank to the back of the wheelchair.

"No problem. Glad to help. Beth, have you met Sheriff Sam Lawson?" Ben asked.

She glanced up and smiled. "I haven't."

The sheriff of Paradise grinned broadly at Beth. "I'd shake your hand, ma'am, but yours are full."

Her smile only widened.

Didn't it figure? Dan shook his head. Oh, yeah, Sam was a charmer, all right. Most of the women in Paradise under the age of eighty were in love with the widowed sheriff. Those who weren't were trying to fix him up with someone.

"Sam, this is my cousin, Dr. Elizabeth Lawson," Ben continued.

When Sam tipped his Stetson, Beth blushed.

Dan was stunned at the zing of jealously that slammed head-on into his gut.

He cleared his throat. "Mom, you go ahead with

Ben and Beth. I'll park the truck, and then Amy and I can find you."

"Okay. And don't worry, Dan, I'm in good hands, remember."

He laughed. "Yeah, I remember, Mom, but I'm not the one who was worried."

He climbed back into the truck and then smiled at his daughter across the cab. Amy's black hair was sticking straight up in places, tangled in others. What would his little girl do without her GG?

Dan took a comb from his pocket and handed it to her. "You start getting the knots out and then I'll braid it for you."

"Daddy, you can't braid."

He shrugged. "I guess you're right. Maybe Dr. Beth will help us out."

Most days, Dan dropped Amy off at his mother's before school, so she could catch the bus at the house. Elsie was the one who fixed her hair each and every morning, and made sure her granddaughter's clothes were "appropriate."

So much of their life was wrapped up in his mother's care. They didn't merely depend on her; they needed her. His mother was their rock. She had been ever since Dan had returned to Paradise with Amy six years ago. Elsie had put aside her own grief at the loss of her husband, and somehow had managed to make everything all right again for Dan and Amy. Life had been all right ever since.

Yeah, he owed his mother a lot.

"Is GG really sick?" Amy asked as she struggled to pull the comb through her dark hair.

"She might be. Remember when you cut your knee? The doctor gave you stitches and medicine and then you came home. Grandma's heart is sick, so they're going to give her medicine and let her rest, and then they'll send her home to get better. Okay?"

With a slow nod, Amy knitted her brows together in fierce concentration.

"What's wrong?" Dan asked.

"What about my program?" she asked in a small voice. "Will GG be able to see me sing?"

"I don't know yet, Pumpkin."

Her lower lip quivered and she closed her eyes. Slow tears began to roll down her little face. "I want GG to come to my program."

Dan put his face close to his daughter's and wiped the tears with his fingers. Then he hugged her. "Amy, I know this is hard. It's hard for me, too, but if we get upset, then GG will get upset. She won't let the doctors help her get better if she's worried about us. I need you to be a brave girl and smile for your grandmother. Tell her she needs to rest and get well again. We can talk about your program when we get home."

Amy sniffed. "Yes, Daddy."

"Thank you, Amy." He glanced at the floor of the

truck. "You'd best grab your backpack. We might be here for a while."

Dan parked the truck and lifted Amy out. They walked hand in hand to the E.R. door. Beth was waiting in the visiting room, pacing back and forth.

The moment she saw Dan and Amy, she smiled, and immediately his heart was warmed. "They've already drawn her blood and taken her straight up for an echocardiogram," she said. "They haven't given her a room number yet, but Ben will text me when they do."

"That was fast," Dan said.

Beth glanced around the E.R. department. "You've got a great facility here. They're really on the ball."

"You're a doctor. I think your presence nudged things along," Dan said.

"It wasn't me, Dan. You have no idea how much respect these people have for you. You should be proud."

"Now I'm embarrassed." He put an arm around his daughter. "Amy, pick a seat and take out your book. I need to talk to Dr. Beth."

Amy sat down and began to dig through her pink backpack.

Dan looked from her to Beth. "Listen, do you mind sitting with Amy for a few minutes? I need to call Joe and let him know what's going on. He'll call the sisters."

"The sisters?" Beth raised her brows.

"Yeah, that's what Joe and I call them." He laughed. "Remind me to tell you about that sometime."

"Okay." Beth smiled. "I think I'll take Amy down to the cafeteria. She hasn't had any breakfast."

"Thanks." He shoved his hands into the pockets of his jeans. "Oh, and I sort of promised that you'd braid her hair." He grimaced, waiting for her response.

"That's not a problem, Dan."

"Thanks." He looked at her, opened his mouth and then closed it again.

"Was there something else?" Beth asked.

"I, uh, heard what you said to my mom, and well, it's probably not a good idea to let her think you're staying."

"But I—"

"Look, Beth, I know your heart is in the right place, but it will be harder in the long run, for everyone, if you let us believe your plans can be changed, when I know they can't."

Beth's eyes flashed with irritation. "*Everyone?* What exactly does that even mean?" she asked.

Dan glanced around the small waiting room, grateful the area was empty. "It means that I care about you, my whole family cares about you, but we're just a stop on the way to New York. We both know that, so it's best not to pretend it's anything else. Right?"

She jerked back. "Pretend? Is that what you think I'm doing?" she fairly hissed. "Pretending?"

"You know what I'm saying, Beth." He'd never seen her really irritated before. But, boy, she was now. Her eyes sparked with fire.

"Oh, yes, I hear you, loud and clear, Mr. Gallagher."

She turned on her heel and walked away from him.

Dan pressed the button on the waiting room beverage machine and watched the paper cup fill with hot, bitter coffee as he mulled over his disastrous conversation with Beth. He'd blown it and he sure didn't know how to make things right.

"Dan."

He turned. "Joe!" Dan moved swiftly across the room to greet his big brother with a man hug.

Joe wore a thick down parka and his right arm hung limply at his side. His green army duffel bag was on the floor next to him.

"How did you get here so fast? It's only been an hour."

Joe laughed. "I was going stir-crazy in that hotel in Denver, so I was already on the road when I got your message. I piggybacked a ride with an old army friend who happens to be a local trucker. He

was headed down 285 anyhow, so he dropped me at
a roadside diner. Then a CDOT pal who was plow-
ing in the area took me straight into town."

"Nice for you."

"How's Mom?" Joe asked.

"Doc's saying she had a mild heart attack. No official word on how much muscle damage due to the
ischemia. They're doing an ultrasound right now.
Then they'll do a balloon angioplasty when the
cardiac specialist gets here."

"You want to translate that medicalspeak to Eng-
lish?"

"What part?" Dan asked. He pulled his coffee
from the vending machine.

"Ischemia. Angio-something."

"She's not getting enough oxygen to her heart.
The procedure they're doing is an angioplasty. They
send a tube into the blocked vessel and then blow
it up a bit like a balloon, and it works like a snowplow to clear the artery."

Joe nodded. "This is a good thing?"

"Yeah. Heart attacks are caused by blockage.
Blood is having a hard time moving through to feed
the heart oxygen."

"Think that procedure will do the trick?"

"Hope so. When all the tests are done we'll know
more."

"When can she come home?"

"Are you kidding? We aren't that far in the discussions yet," Dan said. "We only got here a little while ago. It's surprising everything is happening as fast as it is."

"Wow. Okay. I guess I'll stop with the twenty questions then."

"Thank you," Dan said.

"I called the sisters."

The sisters. Twins Rachel and Leah. Older than Dan and younger than Joe. They worried as much as their mother, and talked twice as much. Only Joe could rein them in.

"Bet that was fun," Dan commented with a chuckle.

"Yeah. Like herding cats by way of a conference call."

Dan laughed.

"They're driving together. Rented a car and are leaving today. They'll be here Saturday afternoon at the earliest."

"Are they bringing the grands?"

"No, I managed to talk them out of that. Told them Mom is recuperating. Six grandkids in one house might be a little much."

"You think?" Dan shook his head. "We can at least hold off the three-ring circus until Saturday, because once they arrive Mom won't rest. You know she'll be trying to take care of everyone."

"True that."

"How are the roads from Gunbarrel?" Dan asked.

"Improving. Why? Are you going someplace?"

"Could be taking a friend to the airport Thursday morning. Not sure yet."

"A friend, huh? Maybe you'll get lucky and the sun will decide to come out today and clear up those roads for you. Oh, and hey, funny thing. I saw a truck in the parking lot that looked exactly like mine. But that's nuts, right?" Joe asked.

Dan shot him a sheepish grin. "Mine is in a ditch."

"You're driving mine because you couldn't keep yours out of a ditch?"

"No, I'm driving your truck because we needed to fit four of us in one vehicle along with all the medical equipment for Mom."

"Four? You brought Millie?"

"We've got company at Mom's place. I was taking Ben Rogers's cousin to Gunbarrel when that blizzard hit on Saturday. She's staying at the ranch until her flight out on Thursday."

"She? So you're even more outnumbered than usual, huh? I'll bet you're real glad the cavalry is back."

Dan laughed. "See, I knew you'd get it."

"How are the cows?"

"Sorry you missed the bulk of the calving."

"Yeah. Too bad, huh?" A wicked gleam appeared in Joe's dark eyes. He slapped Dan on the back. "You lose any?"

"You think I'm a rookie? No. But we do have a twin birth and bonding issues."

"Not your fault. Though I'd blame you if I could figure out a way." Joe grinned.

"Thanks," Dan said.

"Seriously, thank you, Dan."

"I had help. Beth did a lot of work."

"Beth?"

"Yeah. Our houseguest. Her name is Beth." Dan paused, then continued on. "Did the last check on everything around 1:00 a.m. I've got Deke Andrews stopping by to look in on things before he drives to work today."

"Great. Sounds like you've got everything under control." Joe glanced around. "Where's Amy?"

"Having breakfast in the cafeteria with Beth last I checked."

"Beth again. Tell me about this Beth."

Dan shrugged. "Nothing to tell. She's Ben's cousin. An internal medicine physician on her way to a position in New York City."

"Nothing to tell? You have a woman staying at Mom's house and you're going to try to convince me there's nothing to tell?"

"Yeah, that's right."

"Uh-huh."

Dan took a sip of coffee and shuddered. "Nasty."

"So why are you drinking that stuff? Let's go

down to the cafeteria and get some real food. I'd like to meet your Beth. And I miss my niece."

"She's not my Beth." Dan reached for Joe's duffel.

"I've got the bag. I'm not an invalid."

"Hey, did I say that?" Dan asked.

Joe chuckled. "I'm only giving you grief, buddy."

"Thanks, 'cause I missed that while you were gone."

They started down the hall. Dan pressed the elevator button and turned to his brother. "Uh, Joe, maybe I should warn you."

"About what?"

"Beth is not real happy with me right now."

Joe laughed long and hard. "You always did have a way with women."

"Funny, Joe. Real funny."

It was even worse than Dan had expected. Beth and Joe hit it off as if they'd been friends all their lives. Dan sat stirring his coffee and fighting off the morose cloud that hung over him, while they dominated the conversation and Amy colored in her books.

Something had changed Joe, and Dan suspected that it had to do with the trip to Denver. Why, he'd almost suspect there was a woman involved. Well, he'd find out eventually. With Joe, you had to have patience. He didn't share personal information until he was ready.

At least he didn't used to.

Everything seemed odd, because he sure had lots to talk about with Beth.

Right now Joe was talking about his prosthesis. Maybe because she was a doctor.

"They wanted me to start the process post-op, but I wasn't there mentally," he continued.

Beth nodded and Dan stared. How come Joe had never mentioned this before?

"Where is your amputation?" Beth asked.

"Transradial." Joe pointed to the location, right below his elbow on his right arm where the long-sleeved flannel shirt was limp.

"That's actually a positive," she said.

Joe nodded. "Yeah, so they tell me."

"What are your options?" Beth asked.

"Lots of options. In fact, my head is spinning, there are so many. I'm not sure I even remember it all. I was on information overload. There are the cosmetic prostheses and manual ones, and then they have battery operated and what they call hybrid, battery and manual." He pulled a brochure out of his pocket. "I'm excited about these. Look, a myo-electrically controlled one. They use muscle contractions to activate the prosthesis."

"Bionic man?" Dan interjected.

"That's a rather old stereotype," Beth said, her words clipped and flat.

Ouch. She had a mean sucker punch.

Joe's eyes widened a notch, enough to let Dan know he'd caught that.

"Oh, and get this," Joe said. "They even have activity-specific prosthetic devices. I can get one for ranch work."

"This is wonderful, Joe," Beth said.

"So what's the plan now?" Dan asked.

"I had a casting with muscle testing done. I talked to the physician and the therapist. I'll have to work with a therapist here in Paradise, in addition to a couple more fittings in Denver."

"Great," Dan said.

"The myoelectric prosthesis is pretty expensive, so they're trying to get me into a study that will pay for the device."

Beth's phone buzzed. She looked down. "Text from Ben. Your mom has been moved into room 204."

Joe slid from the booth and stood. "So how long are you staying in Paradise, Beth?"

"I changed my flight to Saturday. Amy invited me to her program on Friday, and I've accepted." She glared pointedly at Dan. "Unless you have a problem with that?"

"It's okay, right, Daddy?" Amy asked as she collected her crayons.

Why did he suddenly feel like the bad guy?

"That'd be great." Dan met Beth's gaze. "Thank you, Beth."

Amy's face lit up and she wrapped her arms around Beth, who gave his daughter an affectionate smile, but merely offered him a short nod. He was well aware that he had been dismissed, back to the doghouse.

"Ben offered to take me to the airport if I need a ride," Beth said.

"Oh, I'm sure we can get you to the airport," Joe said, as he stood back for Dan to get out of the booth.

"Thank you." Beth rose to her feet. "Amy and I will meet you boys upstairs." She looked down at Amy again. "We're going shopping."

"Shopping?" Joe asked.

"Yes. To the gift shop to find some barrettes for her hair."

Joe gave a low whistle after Beth had left. "Yeah, you really stepped in it, didn't you?"

"Apparently."

"What did you say?" Joe asked.

Dan felt his ears burning. He shrugged. "It doesn't matter. I thought I was giving her a graceful way out of babysitting the Gallaghers. Turns out she likes us and I insulted her by implying she'd leave us in the lurch."

"Smooth move." Joe bent and gathered his tray. "The question is, how are you going to fix this?"

"She's leaving. Saturday instead of Thursday, but

still leaving, either way. Not much I can do," Dan said as he grabbed the other tray.

"A wise man once said not to dwell on what happened, but to get your apology on the table as fast as you can."

"A wise man?"

"Yeah. Dad. He said that the secret to his and Mom's relationship was that he wasn't afraid to apologize, whether he was right or wrong. Plain and simple."

"Relationship? Do Beth and I even have a relationship?"

"Sounds like you have something." Joe placed his tray on the disposal cart. They walked out of the cafeteria toward the elevator.

"Maybe, but I don't think you get it. Beth is leaving."

"Do you care about her?"

"Well, yeah, but that's beside the point."

"No, little brother, that *is* the point."

"Joe, I—"

Joe raised a hand, effectively cutting Dan off. "It's been six years, dude."

"You sound like Mom now."

"Come on, how many times in six years has someone like Beth wandered into your life?" He didn't give Dan a chance to answer. "You know I'm right."

"Maybe, but how exactly did you get all this

woman wisdom?" Dan asked as he pushed the elevator button.

"Purely from messing up."

"Somehow, that's not real encouraging."

"Look, genius, I'm telling you that you'd better apologize and do it quick. The best thing that's ever happened to you is leaving soon."

Dan ran a hand over his face. He hated when Joe was right.

Chapter Ten

"I'm so glad Joe made it home safely," Elsie said. She sat up in the hospital bed, looking regal, despite being attached to IV, oxygen and cardiac monitoring leads.

"The roads are much better," Beth said.

"So what do you think of my Joe?"

Beth did a mental comparison between the two brothers. Dan was tall and lean and dark, with a nice chin. His older brother was also dark, but with a build like a football player, and not nearly as tall. Dan had that meltingly sweet smile in his favor, along with those clear gray eyes. When he wasn't being a jerk, he was her choice, hands down. "He's very nice," she answered.

"Very PC, dear, but it's obvious you only have eyes for Dan."

"I, um…I like both your sons. You should be proud. You did a fine job raising them, Elsie."

"Thank you." She smiled at the answer. "My girls are coming on Saturday. But after you've gone. I do wish you could have met them. I'm sure they'd love you."

Beth smiled and crossed her arms, unsure what to say.

"Dear, you do know that Dan cares for you, don't you?"

"I'm leaving Saturday," Beth murmured, the admission painful. It wasn't as though she hadn't made it very clear from the beginning. From the very moment she'd met Dan at Ben's house she'd been up-front. She had plans, and a job waiting in New York. Paradise was only a short detour on the road between California and New York. A few more days and she would be gone. That was what she needed to focus on, not the color of Dan's eyes, or the way she felt when he looked at her.

Besides, she had been in Colorado only a week. It was crazy to think she could have developed feelings for Dan Gallagher—or him for her—in such a short amount of time. Crazy! *Right?*

"You know you are always welcome here," Elsie said, still smiling. "If you get to the city and you don't like it as much as Colorado, then you come back. Because, Beth, there's only one thing worse than a bad decision."

She raised her brows in question.

"And that's living with a bad decision."

Beth sighed. Elsie was disturbingly and insightfully correct, as always.

"So, what shall we do about tonight's dinner?" Elsie asked, changing the subject.

"Do you cook dinner every night?" Beth countered.

"Oh, no. I stopped that nonsense years ago. I generally make Sunday dinner after church. I send the boys home with leftovers. Unless Amy is staying with me. I'll cook for my granddaughter, but otherwise, I figure that I've done my time, so to speak. But I do try to keep the freezer stocked for emergencies like this. Do you cook for yourself?" Elsie asked.

"I am quite skilled with a can opener and I can reheat really well."

Elsie chuckled. "That's in your favor, because there happens to be dozens of meals wrapped up and labeled in the freezer, waiting for you to heat up. Pull out the chicken tortilla soup and dump it in a kettle. Amy can show you where everything is," Elsie said.

"Hmm. I'm not exactly confident about the dumping. Amy and I nearly destroyed your kitchen the last time we were allowed to dump," Beth said.

"Now, now. I know you can handle this. It's frozen, so that makes everything slightly safer." Elsie glanced around. "Where is everyone, by the way?"

"They'll be back," Beth said. "Dan took Amy to

see the hospital's nursery. Joe is calling a buddy to get Dan's truck towed from that ditch and brought to the mechanic's shop."

"Good. Where were we?" Elsie cocked her head. "Oh, yes. Soup. They love tortilla soup. All you do is heat it up, then grab a lime and squeeze some in, and add a few chips, some slices of avocado and some Jack cheese. Easy-peasy. Oh, and I've got chicken chili in the freezer also. Now that's a nice meal with a batch of corn bread." She smiled. "Call me if you want me to walk you through it."

"I can check Wikipedia if I need help."

"Wiki what?"

"It's an online encyclopedia."

"Beth, you aren't going to need to look anything up. This is frozen soup we're talking about."

"Don't underestimate my lack of talent in the kitchen. Remember, I'm the one who was confused by cream of tartar."

Elsie laughed and continued. "I think you've got it backward. You're underestimating your abilities. I saw you start that IV. You're good."

"Thank you for having so much confidence in my culinary skills, Elsie, but may I ask a question?"

"Of course, dear."

"Will they deliver pizza to the ranch?"

"Pizza?" Elsie's eyes popped. "Why, it would be stone cold by the time it arrived, and they charge a fortune for the processed stuff. I do, however, have a nice recipe for homemade crust, if you're interested."

"That might be a bit advanced for me."

"Give yourself a little credit, dear. You've got the makings of a good cook. All you lack is some training time. After all, you didn't become a doctor in one day."

"I thought people were either born with the domestic gene or not." Beth shrugged.

"Oh, my. Who told you that? When I married Mr. Gallagher I could barely boil eggs. His dear mother, bless her soul, taught me everything."

"Really? I had no idea. You do it so effortlessly."

"Why, thank you. But the only domestic gene I brought into the marriage was my sense of style." She laughed. "That reminds me. These gowns are plain ugly."

Beth glanced at the white gown with tiny blue flowers. "It's not so bad."

"Ha! Have Dan bring me one of my sweatshirts. The black one that says Dr. Mom in sparkles. It might encourage that fancy cardiac doctor to discharge me."

Amy burst into the room with Dan right behind her.

"GG, I saw the babies." The little girl bounced onto the bed. "They're so tiny. I saw one that was as small as my hand."

"Easy on the bed, Pumpkin." Dan gently scooped

Amy up and deposited her into the bedside chair next to Beth.

"Did you?" Elsie cooed.

Amy nodded. "Yes. I want one."

"You'll have to talk to your daddy about that. He's in charge of bringing you a little brother or sister."

"Mom." Dan's ears reddened.

"What?" Elsie raised her hands to claim her innocence as she turned to Beth. "Do you like babies, Beth?"

"Yes. I'm godmother to Sara and Ben's twins."

"I'm sure you'd make a wonderful mother."

Dan cleared his throat. "*Mom,* Joe will be up here shortly. I'm headed back to the ranch. I'll be back tonight. I'm going to drop Beth off at the ranch first."

"Aren't you going to sleep?" Elsie asked.

"Yeah. I'll stop at my place and take a nap."

Elsie turned to Beth. "Do you mind if Amy stays with you at my house?"

"Mom, Beth doesn't have to—"

"I'd love that. Amy and I can have another piano lesson."

Little Amy nodded enthusiastically.

"Appreciate it," Dan muttered, not meeting her gaze.

"You do not have to come back, Daniel. I'll be fine. Look at all these monitors. If I pass wind they know it."

Beth held in a laugh. Barely.

"I want to come back. Joe and I agreed that one of us would stay with you at night. I'll trade with him later this afternoon."

"Now, that's ridiculous," Elsie said. "This is a hospital. They get paid to take care of me."

"Joe and I specialize in ridiculous, and that's what we're doing."

"Fine. Seems like a waste of your time, but who am I to complain? You know they did say that if the medication continues to work, I might go home tomorrow—"

Beth interrupted. "That would be a very loose interpretation of what you were told. They're going to do the angioplasty later today and the stress test tomorrow, and they might let you go home on Friday. The cardiac doctor said he'd like you to stay until Friday morning rounds, since you live so far out in the country."

"Whose side are you on?" Elsie grumbled.

Beth bit her lip at the look of indignation on Elsie's face.

The silence stretched for a long minute. Finally, Elsie turned to her. "Do you want that pizza recipe before you go?"

"Thank you, but if there isn't home delivery, the soup will be fine. Making pizza from scratch seems a bit ambitious for my skill set."

"You can't go wrong with soup, dear."

Beth shook her head. "Unless there's a drive-through fast-food restaurant that lures me in first."

Dan laughed. "This is Paradise. There's nothing fast in Paradise. That's part of our charm."

Beth thought it was wise to keep her mouth firmly closed.

Someone was watching her. Beth looked up. Dan was peeking his head into the kitchen from the hallway. The twenty-four-hour beard on his face only made him appear even more ruggedly handsome. She glanced away.

I am still mad at him, she reminded her forgiving nature.

"Nothing to worry about," she finally said aloud, her tone dry. "We haven't blown anything up today. Right, Amy?"

Amy giggled and waved at her father from her position at the kitchen table. She knelt on a chair and very carefully stirred brownie batter in a plastic mixing bowl.

"What are you two doing?" Dan asked.

"We're making brownies," Amy said. "I have to mix the batter one hundred times."

"Wow," he replied, coming over and giving his daughter a kiss on the cheek. "All by yourself? I'm impressed."

"GG said we have a teachable spirit, when we called and asked what 'fold in' means."

To his credit Dan only smiled. "Well, GG would know. She taught me to cook," he said.

"Daddy can make lots of stuff," Amy said to Beth.

No doubt he was a much better cook that she was. Beth gave Amy a benevolent smile but offered nothing to the conversation.

Yes, she was still irritated at Dan for his hurtful comment at the hospital. Of course, the situation was totally her own fault. This was what happened when you got too close to people. You got hurt.

Dan stuck a finger in the bowl and tasted the batter. "Good stuff, Amy."

"Daddy, GG says we can't eat the batter or we might get sick."

"Not to contradict your grandmother, Pumpkin, but I've eaten batter all my life and never once got sick," he said.

"What does *contradict* mean?" Amy asked.

"It means I'm a bad example. Listen to your grandmother," he said.

Amy frowned at him and wiped a bit of chocolate batter off her fingers with a paper towel. "Look, Daddy, I got my nails done today. Dr. Beth polished them for me. My nails match hers now."

"Whoa, they sure do." He glanced at Beth's pale pink nails and then at his daughter's. "You look beautiful, just like Dr. Beth."

Beth concentrated on wiping a spot of batter from

the table with her dishcloth. She refused to be lured by compliments, no matter how sweet.

When she straightened, the distinct scent of tomatoes with a hint of oregano and mozzarella cheese drifted past. "Do you smell something?" she asked Amy.

"No," Amy said. "Just brownies."

"Well, I do." She sniffed again and walked around the kitchen. "It's almost like…"

"Pizza?" Dan asked.

Beth whirled around. "Yes. That's exactly what I smell." She turned to him and narrowed her eyes. "Did you bring home pizza?"

"Yeah, I heard you mention it to my mother."

"Daddy! Pizza?" Amy exclaimed.

"Uh-huh. Go wash your hands."

"What about the brownies, Dr. Beth?"

"I'll put them in the oven. You go ahead." Beth slid a spatula into the bowl and began pouring the batter into a square glass pan.

Dan left the room and returned with two pizza boxes, and Millie following closely behind. He set the boxes onto the table. "Look, Beth," he began. "I was completely off base—"

She walked over to the oven, opened the door and placed the pan on the top rack, allowing the door to slam shut in the middle of his half-baked apology.

"I'm trying to apologize." He cleared his throat. "For what I said at the hospital. I know you care about all of us, and I appreciate that you changed your reservations to help us out. I hope you can forgive me for opening my big mouth."

"You're apologizing with pizza?" she asked, hoping her expression clearly screamed, *not really!*

"I brought your luggage, too."

Okay, this time she was unable to resist a slight roll of her eyes.

"Could you work with me here? It was the best I could do on short notice."

The doorbell rang and they both turned toward the sound.

"I'll heat the pizza up if you want to get the door," she said.

He shook his head. "No, I don't care about the door. I want to know if you'll accept my apology."

"Pepperoni?" she asked, peeking into the top box.

"Yes. One with Canadian bacon, too."

"Okay. Fine. Yes. I forgive you."

He shoved his hands into his pockets. "Boy, that sounded convincing."

"What exactly are you looking for here? An award or something?"

"Could I have a hug?"

"A *hug?*" Beth stepped back from him. "Is that necessary?"

"It really is. An old-fashioned Gallagher 'get out of the doghouse' tradition."

Beth looked at him as she considered his request,

and then glanced away. "That seems like a very awkward tradition."

"Not much of a hugger?"

She shook her head. "Not a hugger, period."

"You let Amy hug you," he returned.

"Amy is only half a person and she sort of catches me off guard. Besides, I've gotten used to her."

"Maybe you could get used to me, too."

Beth released a shaky breath. She doubted she could ever get used to Dan's touch.

Silence stretched.

"Fine. If it will make you feel better."

"It will, and don't worry, I'll do all the work." Dan gently wrapped his big arms around her, tucked her head under his chin and hugged.

He was warm and solid, and she could hear the steady beat of his heart. For a brief moment she relaxed and sort of hugged him back.

Yes, hugs were nice.

But you're leaving. You're leaving. The words sounded over and again in her head.

I know.

When he stepped back, Beth was surprised at how much chillier the room seemed without his comforting warmth.

"Thank you, Beth," he said softly.

"I, uh, you're welcome." She turned away quickly, picked up the mixing bowl and placed it in the sink, then turned on the water.

"I'm sorry for questioning your motives. I guess I'm still carrying around more baggage than I realized," Dan said. "It was your basic knee-jerk reaction. I was being a jerk and trying to protect myself."

"From what? I would never purposely hurt you. We're friends. Right?" she asked as she scrubbed at the bowl.

"Beth, I care for you. More than I realized. No matter when you leave, it's going to hurt."

She stopped and didn't move, more than a little stunned at his admission and not willing to admit that she felt the same way.

The doorbell rang again, this time with a pounding on the wooden door.

"Dan?" a female voice called out.

"Emily?" he asked, moving out of the kitchen and down the hall.

Emily the midwife. Beth moved to the doorway, unable to resist listening to the conversation.

"Hey, Dan, I heard about your mother. I thought maybe you could use some nourishment."

Emily had brought food. Of course. Why not? Everyone could cook but Beth.

"Come on in, Em. Do you want me to take that?"

"If you'll point me to the kitchen I can carry it in," she said sweetly.

"Uh, right down here."

Racing to the sink, Beth shoved her hands back in the soapy water.

"This is so nice. Homey. You did a great job decorating. Love the stainless steel."

"Um, Emily, I didn't decorate. This is my mom's place. Amy and I have a house down the road."

"Why didn't I know that?" The woman's laughter filled the kitchen.

"You can place it on the counter," Dan said. "Sure looks good."

"Oh, I didn't realize you were still here," Emily said, her voice a tad less confident. "I thought I heard planes were taking off again at the airport."

Beth turned around and met her curious gaze. "No. I'm still here. I'm staying another couple of days, since Elsie is in the hospital."

"That's really nice of you."

"We were about to have pizza," Dan said. "Do you want to join us?"

"I don't want to intrude, and I need to get going, anyhow." Emily peeled back the foil from the casserole. "This will go great with pizza. It's my special lasagna recipe." She looked up at Dan through her lashes like a lovesick puppy. "I hope you like homemade lasagna."

Beth glanced away. Was he truly oblivious to Emily's feelings? How could he be when they were written all over the other woman's face?

"Love it," Dan said. "Thank you."

"You're welcome." Emily smiled and stepped closer to him. "Are you planning on going to the big bake sale in town next week?" she asked quietly.

"I haven't thought that far out." He offered a weak smile. "Things have been a little crazy."

"It's the Paradise Ladies Auxiliary fund-raiser for the library. If you decide to go, let me know and I'll save you a ticket."

He nodded and swallowed. "I'll do that."

Amy walked into the room waving her clean hands in front of him. "Pizza now, Daddy?"

"In a minute. Say hi to Miss Emily."

"Hi, Miss Emily," Amy parroted.

"She's so cute." Emily placed a hand on Dan's arm. "So I'll see you in church on Sunday?"

"Oh, yeah. Sure."

"Nice to see you again, Beth. When did you say your flight was?"

"Saturday."

"And where's home?"

"I'm headed to New York City," Beth said as she dried her hands again.

"Wow. New York. The biggest city I've been to is Denver. I guess I'm just a country girl at heart." She turned to share the wattage of her smile and bat her baby blues at Dan.

"Let me walk you out," he said.

"That would be lovely." Emily shot a little smile into the air near Beth. "Bye. Best of luck."

"Thanks," Beth replied.

"Daddy, can we *please* eat?" Amy called. "I'm starving."

"Sure, Pumpkin, you go ahead. I'll be along in a bit."

"Pizza for you, Amy, or lasagna?" Beth asked.

"I want pepperoni pizza. Lots of pepperoni pizza."

"Atta girl," Beth said as she flipped open the pizza box.

Emily's voice trailed down the hall. "Do you have a second to look at my engine? It's been making funny noises."

"Sure. Let me get my toolbox."

Beth grabbed a dish and silverware for Amy and put a thick slice of pizza on the plate.

"Aren't you eating?" Amy asked.

"Not right now," Beth said. Her appetite had vanished the moment Dan and Emily left the room.

Was she jealous? Maybe. One thing was clear: Emily was smart and pretty, she cooked, *and* she was a country girl. The only thing unclear was what Dan was waiting for.

Chapter Eleven

Dan pulled open the barn door and stepped back, surprised to find his brother inside mucking out the stalls.

"What are you doing here? You were going to stay at the hospital with Mom today," Dan said.

"I got kicked out. The Ladies Auxiliary took over the room. Thursday is Bible study and they decided to move it to Mom's room rather than have it without her. Bitsy Harmony is going to stay with her until tonight."

"So much for your bonding time with Mom."

Joe laughed. "That's Dr. Mom to you."

"How'd you get home?" Dan asked.

"Sheriff Lawson dropped me off." He nodded to the workstation. "They sent me home with homemade pastries, so I can't complain. Besides, it could be worse. They could have wanted me to stay."

"Good point." Dan opened the box. "Were you going to eat them all?"

"No. But I got distracted and haven't made it up to the house with yours yet."

"There are at least a dozen in here. You were only going to save me one?"

"I'm bigger than you. I need more nourishment."

Dan scoffed as he looked Joe up and down. He grabbed a Danish and bit in, licking his lips. "Cheese. These are amazing. Looks like we underestimated the value of Mom's church ladies."

"I'll say," Joe answered.

"Did you hear anything about the results of the angioplasty?" Dan asked.

"Well, I'm not a medical professional like you and Beth, but I translated the doctorspeak to mean that the procedure was successful. They're going to put her on some meds to keep the arteries clear."

"Good news, all the way around," Dan said as he lifted a second Danish from the box. "So, how can I help you today?"

"You're a bottomless pit, aren't you? Finished off the pizza the other night and the lasagna. By the way, that was good lasagna."

"Emily Robbs brought it."

"You've got women falling over you, left and right," Joe observed.

"Too bad I'm not interested," Dan said.

"Seriously? What's your problem? Are you going to let one mistake color your whole life?"

"This isn't about me. Every decision I make affects Amy."

Joe shook his head. "Don't you think maybe it's time you faced your fears instead of blaming everything on Amy?"

"You know what MYOB means?"

"Whatever," Joe said. Suddenly, his ears perked up. "You hear the phone ring?"

"No." Dan stared at his brother. This was curious. "Who are you expecting a call from?"

He shrugged. "Physical therapist."

"Anyone I know?"

"Nope. And let's keep it that way."

"*Female.* You're waiting for a call from a woman." Dan nearly dropped the Danish.

"I said it was a therapist."

Dan shoved the rest of the flakey pastry into his mouth and eyed the remaining golden treats. "A therapist who is a woman. That's what you said."

"No. You said that." Joe closed the white box and handed him the pitchfork. "Go do something constructive."

Dan started tossing hay. "You *could* call *her*," he said.

"It's her move."

"I knew it was a woman."

Joe glared over the wooden rails at him. "Are you still here?"

The phone rang and they both jumped toward the

sound, shouldering each other aside and then practically wrestling for the portable's handset. It fell to the ground and bounced. Joe dived for the receiver and barely managed to yank it out of Dan's grasp.

"Hello?" he panted. "Yeah. Okay. I'll tell him. Thanks," he said to the caller.

"For me?" Dan asked as he picked up the pitchfork.

"That was the garage," Joe muttered. "Your truck is ready."

"That was fast."

"We've been snowed in for five days. I imagine they're twiddling their thumbs."

"You want to drive me in to Paradise?" Dan asked.

"I guess I could," Joe said slowly. He glanced at his watch. "Maybe."

"What do you mean, maybe?"

"Hey, you know what? I've got an idea," Joe continued.

"Trying to scare me?"

Joe ignored him. "Why don't I spend some time with my niece? Amy and I can see a Disney movie in town and then I'll buy her a burger and a strawberry milkshake at the Prospector."

"That's your big idea?"

"Yeah. I need to—" He cleared his throat. "I want to hit the noon matinee. Think you can have her ready to go in time?"

"Sure."

"Great. And you know, Beth has been here nearly a week and has been stuck on the ranch. This would be the perfect time to show her Paradise."

"I don't know...." Dan stared at the hay.

"She still mad at you?"

"No, and I'd like to keep it that way."

"How can you get in trouble showing her around town?"

Dan met his brother's gaze. "Trust me, if there's a road leading straight to a cow patty, I'll find it."

Joe laughed. "What kind of logic is that? Beth's been an unpaid ranch hand for five days. The least you can do is take her to town. Show her your pharmacy, and Patti Jo's Café and that crazy shop where Mom buys all her sweatshirts."

"I guess. Seems harmless enough."

"Sure it is."

"Why do I think you're trying to distract me from what's really going on here?" Dan leaned on the pitchfork and assessed his brother. "Let's back up a minute. Why are you all jacked up about taking Amy to a movie?"

"I told you. I want to spend some quality time with my niece."

"You have to be at the noon matinee to do that?"

Joe pulled off his ball cap and then slapped it back on.

Dan's eyes widened as it finally hit him. "Are you meeting someone at the movie?"

"Well, if I sort of run into someone, that would be a nice coincidence." Joe paused. "She has a daughter Amy's age."

"She?" Dan burst out laughing. "Your therapist?"

"Stop laughing."

"You set me up." Dan shook his head. "You had this all planned."

"Not really. I ran into my therapist on the way out of the hospital and we talked about getting the kids together. She said something about taking her daughter to the noon matinee. I was sort of hoping for an opening so I could ask you." He had the grace to look sheepish. "Everything fell into place on its own."

"Oh, the mighty, how they fall."

"What's that supposed to mean?" Joe muttered.

"Nothing. Not a thing. What's with the phone call?"

"She was supposed to call me and let me know for sure if she was going to be at the movie."

"I was right—you already made plans for my daughter."

"Amy likes Disney movies." Joe shrugged. "I don't see what the problem is."

"What if Amy couldn't go?"

"I hadn't thought that far ahead." Joe glanced at

his watch again. "You're really going to make me work for this, aren't you?"

"Have you considered just asking this gal out to dinner?"

Joe blinked as though considering those words. "Naw. My way is less threatening."

"For who?" Dan asked.

"Look, everyone knows that the way to a woman's heart is through her kid."

Dan slapped his forehead. "Oh, man. Tell me again why I'm taking advice from you?" Not that he needed advice. Because he didn't. Advice on romancing a woman was of no use to a man who wasn't looking for romance. Especially not with another woman who was counting the days until she'd leave him behind.

Dan stood in the doorway watching Beth and Amy. Their backs were to him as they sat on the living room couch. He should be reading with Amy, but instead Beth was, and she was doing a much better job than he ever did. The woman had endless patience.

"What's that word?" Amy asked.

Beth bent closer, picked up Amy's finger and put it on the word. "Now, try it a little at a time."

"El…"

"Yes," Beth encouraged.

"E…"

"E sounds like *uh* here."

"Pant?" She glanced up at Beth.

"*Ph* makes the *f* sound."

"Elephant!" Amy exclaimed.

"Very good."

Amy leaned affectionately into Beth, who smiled down at her and brushed the bangs from Amy's eyes.

Dan's heart filled and he swallowed the lump in his throat. His mother was correct, Beth would make a good mother…in New York City, or wherever she finally settled down.

"Afternoon, ladies."

"Daddy." Amy turned and put down her book. "Did you visit GG today?"

"Uncle Joe did and the Paradise Ladies Auxiliary is keeping her company right now."

"I miss her."

"Me, too, Pumpkin, but she'll be home soon."

"Tomorrow for my program?"

"I don't know yet."

Amy nodded solemnly. "Dr. Beth and I picked out our clothes for the program. She's going to braid my hair and tie ribbons on the end."

"I know you're going to look beautiful."

Beth twisted around on the couch and met his gaze. She smiled. A genuine, survived-the-hug-and-lived-to-tell-about-it smile. Dan swallowed hard against the emotion stirring within him.

"So, Amy, Uncle Joe wants to take you out for a Disney movie and a cheeseburger. He's meeting a friend who has a little girl your age."

"Do I know her?"

"Probably not, but it's always fun to make new friends, right?"

Amy sighed. "Sometimes it's scary, but if Uncle Joe is with me I guess it will be okay."

"Uncle Joe is lots of fun," Dan said. "Why don't you go get ready? We'll leave here shortly."

He turned to Beth. "Dr. Beth, how would you like to see Paradise? I have to pick up my truck at the garage and then we can go tour the big town."

"That would be really nice." Her eyes widened and a slow smile warmed her face.

"But there's a catch," Dan said.

She cocked her head. "What's that?"

"I don't want to talk about the fact that you're leaving Saturday morning. Don't want to think about it. Deal?" Their gazes locked.

"Deal," Beth said softly.

Beth turned her head at the sound of shovels hitting cement. Merchants were clearing the sidewalks of Paradise, ridding the pavement of the snow that was piled up everywhere.

"Hey, careful." Dan took her arm and pulled her close to him.

He nodded toward the large pothole puddle she had nearly stepped in.

"Thanks."

"No problem." His warmth and strength touched Beth as he held her arm until they had safely crossed the street.

"What did you think of the pharmacy?" he asked.

"It's cute."

"Beth, it's a pharmacy, it's not supposed to be cute."

"I'm sorry, but it is. It looks like an old-time apothecary. How long has that place been open?"

"As long as Paradise has been around."

"I rest my case." She looked up at him. "I'll bet they're missing you while you've been off."

"They owe me something like three years' worth of days off. They'll survive. This will make them appreciate me." He glanced down. "Do you still have the bag?"

"Yes. I put it in my purse."

"My mother is going to love that sweatshirt."

"I hope you're right. I would have never guessed that a sequined sweatshirt with the words I Put the B in Subtle would make anyone happy."

"You have to think like my mother." He chuckled.

"When did your mom start collecting those... quirky shirts?"

"I don't know. She's been wearing them as long

as I remember. I'm just grateful she doesn't wear them to church."

"Her church friends are with her today at the hospital?"

"Yeah. Paradise Ladies Auxiliary. Sort of an interdenominational group, comprised of all the church ladies in the area. Kind of a cross between a Bible study and philanthropic group."

"I see."

Across the street a group of elderly women called Dan's name and waved. He waved back.

"More of my mother's church friends."

"Do you and your family go to church every Sunday?"

"Pretty much."

She frowned, confused. "Why?"

"I go because the Bible says to. I also go because church grounds me. Time in church prepares me for another week. It soothes my soul, and helps me remember why I'm here. To serve Him. Everything else is icing."

"I've never really thought about why I'm here."

"Maybe you should."

Beth stiffened at the words. Of course it wasn't an insult, but it was like a splash of cold water. Why *was* she here?

"Maybe you should drop into a church and sit for a while, let His presence seep into your soul. Then you can ask for yourself."

"That's all there is to it?"

"He's a polite God. He'll never go where He's not wanted. The Lord is waiting for you to welcome Him into your heart. Then He'll direct you."

She nodded, captivated by the explanation. "Thank you. No one has ever explained things to me like that."

"Anytime, Beth." Dan took her arm again. "Whoa. Ice." He pointed to the sidewalk and they walked around the patch.

"What's that wonderful smell?" Beth asked as they came to an intersection and then crossed the street again.

Dan grinned. "Cookies."

"Cookies?" She looked around the town square, where a series of quaint shops surrounded a charming little park.

"Patti Jo's Café and Bakery. And it's Thursday." He stopped in the middle of the sidewalk and inhaled, then nodded. "Yep. Oatmeal cinnamon raisin."

"You can tell by the smell?"

"Oh, yeah. And these are not your ordinary cookies. People come from all over for Patti Jo's cookies. The oatmeal cinnamon raisin are big and really soft, and frosted with a lemon icing."

"Lemon?" Beth murmured the word and licked her lips. "I like lemon."

"We could stop. Looks like we could get a window seat, too. During peach season you can't even get in the door. The lines are down the street for Patti Jo's peach pies and cobblers. And after all, Patti Jo's is a historical site."

"How can that be?" Puzzled, Beth pointed to the print on the window. "It says established in 2005."

"This is where Sara and Ben met."

Beth laughed. "Oh, well then, yes. We had better stop."

Dan pulled open the crimson front door, setting off the welcome tinkle of the shop's bells.

The bakery was wonderfully predictable. Up front, old-fashioned stainless steel and glass cases were filled with breads and pastries. Behind the counter were more shelves that held row after row of cookies.

A chalkboard on the wall declared, as Dan had predicted, oatmeal cinnamon raisin as the cookie of the day. A dozen for six dollars, which seemed a bit overpriced until Beth glanced at the cookies. Golden brown with a light yellow glaze, they were the size of saucers.

She followed him to a table with red vinyl stools set close to a window, which provided an unobstructed view of the park and the gazebo.

"How many?" he asked, with a nod toward the cases of treats.

"I'll take one," Beth said.

"One? You must be kidding."

She laughed. "I can't eat two. They're enormous."

He raised his brows. "They're two for a dollar. Seems a waste to order one."

"Get two for me and I'll take one back for Amy."

"Good idea." Dan grinned. "Coffee?"

"Yes, please."

"Black, right?"

She nodded.

He moved through the shop to the counter, greeting the few customers along the way. It was obvious he was liked and respected. No doubt he knew every single person in Paradise.

What would it be like to fit into a town like Paradise? To live here? To know everyone and be welcomed? Beth mulled over the idea, surprised that the more she thought about it, the more it appealed to her.

A young waitress followed him back to the table, setting a plastic tray with coffee and two bags of cookies down.

"Thanks, Carly."

"No problem, Mr. Gallagher."

"Ouch," he murmured as he put a stack of napkins in the middle of the table. "She called me Mr. Gallagher."

"That's how I feel when the grocery baggers call me ma'am," Beth said.

He slid her coffee and a bag of cookies across the table. "Are we getting old?"

"I think we still have a few good years left," she answered.

"How old are you?" Dan asked.

"Thirty-one. How old are you?"

"I'll be thirty-two next month."

"Oh, well," Beth said. "I had no idea you really were old, when I spoke."

He nodded. "You're getting good with the zingers."

"Thank you." She pulled a cookie out of the bag and took a bite. "Uh-oh."

Dan raised his brows.

"I think I might have a new addiction."

He laughed. "Yep. They are that good."

She gave a short nod as she took another bite and swallowed. "What's that statue in the middle of the park?"

"Founder's statue. The Paradise Ladies Auxiliary funded that. It's a bronzed relief map of Colorado, with a star to show Paradise and the date in 1871 when we were officially founded and added to the state map."

"Of course."

"That's not all. We have a Founder's Day celebration every spring, third weekend in June. Biggest event of the year."

June. She'd be settled in New York by then. *One thousand nine hundred thirteen miles away.* She had checked the distance on her tablet computer last night.

Both Dan and Beth turned as a family with a toddler and an infant filled the booth next to them.

"What is it about babies?" Dan said. "They lull you into thinking you want a houseful."

"Do you?" Beth asked. She took another bite of cookie and looked up at him.

"Yeah, I guess I do," Dan said with a musing smile. "I mean, I sure don't want Amy to be an only child." His gaze met Beth's. "What about you?"

"Oh, I've never really thought about it."

"I don't buy that. Everybody thinks about it at some point or another."

"I'm not everybody." She sighed. "Besides, I'm really not very experienced with kids."

"Amy really likes you."

"I really like Amy."

"No. I mean she *really* likes you."

"Oh, she's just clingy because she misses her grandmother."

Dan looked at Beth over the rim of his coffee cup. "I've said this before, but you're awfully hard on yourself."

"I like to think I'm realistic."

"Realistic. What does that mean?"

She played with the napkin "It means that I am aware that I come with a lot of baggage."

"A lot of baggage you keep locked in the attic. Have you considered tossing everything away and starting over?"

"What do you mean?"

"Ever see that bumper sticker? It's Never Too Late to Have a Happy Childhood."

"Easy to say. You *had* a happy childhood."

"Yeah, and so can you. You started to have fun and let it all go here in Paradise. Don't stop now. Give yourself permission to be a kid."

"You don't understand. I've spent so much of my life living one day at a time…." She swallowed, unable to continue.

"You don't have to live like that anymore." He took her hands.

Beth stiffened for a moment before relaxing. This was Dan. She could trust Dan.

"What are you afraid of?" he asked quietly.

"I'm not afraid."

"Sure you are. You're terrified. What happened?"

"Happened?"

"Is there something you haven't told me?"

She couldn't meet his eyes; instead, she slipped her hands from his and began to twist the napkin into a rope. "I wasn't completely truthful with you about my mother."

"Go ahead. It's okay."

"I did talk to her. Face-to-face. I'm sorry I didn't

mention it. But you know, I didn't think we'd become…well, you know…"

"Friends?"

"Yes." Beth nodded. She took a deep breath. "My mother told me I was a mistake. She begged me not to tell her new family." Beth blinked and looked down at the table. She hadn't cried since she was twelve. She wasn't going to start now. "My own mother didn't even want to acknowledge me, outside of telling me to never contact her again."

Dan's jaw tightened. "I'm sorry. Sorry for her loss. But remember that there are plenty of people who care for you. Unconditionally."

Her eyes widened.

"Ben, Sara, Amy, my mother. Me."

Unconvinced, Beth couldn't help but frown.

"Beth, you need to understand that what your mother did is not a reflection on you as a person. You are no less amazing in my eyes and, more important, in the Lord's."

She sat very still, overwhelmed by his words.

"Eventually you'll get to the place where you can forgive your mother and move on."

"That seems unlikely."

"Letting go isn't easy, but it sure makes life a lot more enjoyable."

Wordless, Beth could only stare at Dan. His soft gray eyes told her he was sincere, but she couldn't wrap her mind around what he was saying.

"Always remember that your past is just that. You should learn from your past, not live there."

"That's pretty deep."

"I'm quoting the Bible."

Beth cocked her head. "That's in the Bible?"

"Yeah. Philippians 3:13. 'Forgetting those things which are behind and reaching forth unto those things which are before.'"

"You memorized the verse?"

His ears reddened. "Paraphrased. That's sort of my personal mantra. I generally fall short of living up to the words. But you know..." he shrugged "...I try."

As he made the admission, Beth realized that she was falling in love with the man across the table from her. A small gasp slipped from her lips.

"You okay?" He peered into her face.

"Yes. Yes, I'm fine." She smiled and shook her head.

"Ready to go?" he asked.

Beth nodded.

"Did Ben show you the memorial gardens at the clinic?"

"No. We didn't have enough time," she said.

"It's an amazing place. Ben and Sara were married there. We'll stop there next."

"We're really seeing everything, aren't we?" Beth asked.

"I want you to see all you'll be leaving behind."

"Oh, I know exactly what I'll be leaving behind," she murmured, her heart overflowing. She wasn't sure if she should be happy or sad at the revelation that she'd fallen in love with Daniel Gallagher.

Chapter Twelve

"Hey, Beth, the Ladies Auxiliary is gone. Come on in here. Mom is going to tell us about her adventures in hospital-land."

Beth hurried into the kitchen and sat down in the empty chair on the other side of Elsie. Both Dan and Joe had come in from their chores to greet their newly returned mother and eat lunch.

Elsie patted Beth's hand. "The house looks immaculate. Thank you. My friends were so impressed."

"I put Amy in charge." Beth shrugged. "It was actually fun."

Dan leaned over to his mother. "Beth has some strange ideas about fun, but we're working on her."

"Tell us about the hospital, GG," Amy said as she dumped out her crayon box on the table.

"Oh, my, let me think. This has been quite a week, hasn't it?" She looked at Dan. "What day is it, anyhow?"

"It's Friday. Do I need to do a neuro exam on you, Mom?"

"No, smarty, I've just lost track of the days from being out of my usual routine, that's all." She grinned. "Paradise Hospital is very nice. Everyone is so polite. They have flat-screen televisions in all the rooms." She turned to Beth. "Oh, and the staff wear such cute scrubs. You'd love working there."

Beth chewed her lip. She'd never spent so much time trying not to laugh. Today Elsie wore the shirt Dan and Beth had purchased yesterday, the flashy, sequined, I Put the B in Subtle one. She looked like herself again. Her color was back and she glowed in the presence of her adoring family.

Beth had to admit that she, too, adored Elsie, certainly more than her real mother.

"Did you happen to see Sara's uncle Henry?" Dan asked with a wiggle of his brows.

"Uncle Henry?" Beth asked, looking from Dan to Elsie.

"Dr. Rhoades," Dan said. "Didn't you meet him when you toured the hospital with Ben?"

"Yes. You're trying to hook your mother up with Sara's uncle?"

Dan looked pointedly at Beth. "Maybe you should be wearing Mom's shirt."

"What?" she asked.

"That was *subtle,* Beth." He paused. "Not."

"Oh, you," Elsie said. "Do you suppose a big-shot doctor has time to visit every patient?"

"Did he come by?" Dan prodded.

"As a matter of fact, he did." She blushed. "He was very gentlemanly, and he has a nice smile."

"Ahh, Mom. See? I told you. Dr. Rhoades has a crush on you," Dan said.

"Oh, pooh, I don't believe it for a minute. He was being nice because of Ben."

"Mom," Joe said, his face expressing his impatience. "Could we cut to the chase? What did the doctor say when you were discharged?"

"It was a *mild* heart attack," Elsie said, as she glanced around the kitchen table at her family. "Actually, I feel better than I have in a long time. Apparently, oxygen is much more important than I realized." She shrugged.

Dan shook his head in dismay. *"Apparently?"*

"They said with medication and a modified diet along with exercise, I should be just fine."

"What exactly is a modified diet?" Joe asked.

Elsie shuddered. "I don't even want to think about that right now. As long as it doesn't include those nasty cherry gelatin cubes the hospital serves, I'm sure it will be fine."

Dan chuckled. "Joe, I hate to break it to you, but modified diet means less red meat."

Horror was clearly evident on Joe's face. "Not

seriously? That's crazy. Gallaghers have been raising beef for nearly fifty years."

"Dan, don't tease your brother," Beth said. She
turned to Joe. "A modified diet means lean protein
choices along with more grains, fruits and vegeta-
bles, legumes."

"Thank you, Beth," Joe said. "She can eat lean
beef."

Amy looked up from her coloring. "What's a
lagoon?"

"Legume. *L-E-G-U-M-E,*" Dan said. "A good
word to remember for our word game." He winked
at Beth.

"Legume," Amy drawled. "But what is it?"

"A legume would be a bean or a nut or a pea,"
Beth explained. "In fact, I thought I'd cook some
legumes tonight for Elsie's homecoming dinner.
Along with some nice tofu burgers."

There was silence around the table.

"You're kidding, right?" Dan asked.

"Yes. I am," Beth answered flatly.

He laughed and pointed a finger at her. "*That was
good.* You got me."

She smiled. "I did, didn't I?"

"Very good, Beth." Dan began to clap, and Joe
and Elsie chimed in.

Beth struggled to keep a straight face, eventually
bursting out with a laugh. Life at the Gallaghers'

was fun. Maybe she was falling in love with the whole family and not just Dan.

"Actually, the Ladies Auxiliary brought over a lot of food," Elsie said. "I may not have to cook ever again."

"I saw what Bitsy and the gang brought. Not heart healthy," Dan observed. "Joe and I might be forced to bite the bullet and take it off your hands. Right, Joe?"

"Sacrifice for dear old Mom."

"I am not old."

"No, but you are *dear,*" Joe said. He stood and placed his dish in the sink, and then leaned down to squeeze his mother's shoulders.

Elsie reached up and patted his arm. "Such a good boy, Joseph."

"What about me?" Dan protested.

"I think we can all concur that you are the troublemaker," Joe said.

"I'm Mom's favorite," Dan said with smile.

"Yes. That's true. You are my favorite youngest son."

"Point for Elsie," Beth murmured.

"Okay, come on, Dan. We've got to move that herd to the south pasture. Snow's starting to melt there. You ready?"

"Sure." Dan pushed back his chair and stood. He, too, put his dish in the sink, before grabbing his hat from the back of his chair. "Hey, how was your date yesterday, Joe?"

Joe's head popped up, panic in his eyes. "It wasn't a date, and I don't want to talk about it." He glared at Dan as he shoved his ball cap on his head. "I told you he was a troublemaker," he muttered.

Dan only chuckled. "Ladies, I guess we'll see you tonight for the performance of our star, Miss Amy Pumpkin Gallagher." He bowed, sweeping the air in front of him with his Stetson.

"Da-ddy!"

He flipped Amy's braids over her shoulder and kissed the top of her head before he headed down the hall.

"May I play piano, GG?"

"Yes, you may, sweetheart."

The front door closed and Elsie turned to Beth, her eyes crinkled with amusement. "Now we can talk. How was your trip to town yesterday? Did you have fun?"

"It was very nice."

Elsie frowned. She had obviously hoped for more than simply "nice."

"I, um, especially enjoyed Patti Jo's Café and the memorial garden at the clinic," Beth offered.

"Did you know that Sara and Ben had their wedding in that garden? Several members of the Auxiliary were bridesmaids."

"Really? I love that! I'll have to get Ben to show me the pictures."

"When Ben first came here he was a city boy himself. Good grief, rumor has it that he came with a suitcase and his espresso machine." Elsie looked intently at Beth. "Didn't take him long to fall in love with Paradise."

"That's funny because Ben was raised in the country, and ended up a city kid, like me. But I can understand why he fell in love with Paradise."

"Can you? Paradise really is a wonderful town."

Beth glanced out the window at the white scenery. "I bet it's even more beautiful in the summer."

Elsie's smile got wider. "Why, yes. Paradise really is amazing in the summer months. It doesn't get as hot as Denver, and the nights are still cool. We get lots of tourists and there are so many events going on." She paused and looked at her intently. "Have you thought any more about staying?"

"I have," Beth admitted. "More than once."

"That's a start." Elsie brightened for a moment. "But you're still leaving tomorrow?"

"That's the plan. I hope I don't regret it."

"My mother used to say that regrets are like wishes. Neither one keeps you warm at night."

As she spoke, Elsie's head swayed rhythmically to the sound of the simple melody floating in from the living room. "Goodness, Amy certainly has improved since you arrived. I used to get a headache after she'd finished giving her dolls lessons, but I couldn't bear to tell her she couldn't play. Now it sounds like real music."

"She's a quick learner and she loves to practice. Maybe you could ask Dan about private lessons."

"Wonderful idea. I'll do that."

The music stopped and Amy came back into the kitchen, carrying her doll. She slipped her arms around her grandmother's waist and rested her head against her shoulder. "I'm so glad you're back, GG."

"Thank you, Amy." Elsie stroked her granddaughter's hair. "I heard you had a fun day yesterday."

"Uncle Joe took me to the movies and we had dinner. A cheeseburger and a milkshake."

"Did you meet Uncle Joe's friends?"

"Uh-huh. Miss Claire, she's a therapist, and her daughter. She's little, though. Only four years old."

"Sounds like fun."

"It was good." Amy cocked her head. "Can we get dressed for my program now?"

"Oh, not much longer. You can go and set out clean underwear for your bath." Elsie looked at the brass clock on the kitchen wall. "Look at the time. Beth, will you excuse me? I need to make a few calls about that bake sale next week."

"Sure." Beth put a hand on Elsie's arm and met her gaze. "Promise me that you'll take it easy and maybe have a nap before tonight?"

"Yes, dear, I'll try. It's awfully nice having my own doctor at the house." She reached out and covered Beth's hand. "Thank you," she said. Her eyes were moist and her words heartfelt.

"For what?" Beth asked.

"Dear, you saved my life."

"No—"

Elsie shook her head adamantly. "I know you aren't one to draw much attention to yourself, but you did. It's okay to just say 'you're welcome.' God gave you a gift. So many gifts. We've been so blessed by your presence."

Beth's nose tingled with emotion. She swallowed and turned her head. Outside, in the distance, Joe and Dan sat tall in the saddles of their horses, herding the cattle, with the black-and-white dogs running alongside.

She turned back to Elsie. "You're welcome."

"Pretty exciting, isn't it?" Dan commented to his mother as they found seats in the elementary school auditorium on Friday night. The room was abuzz with the excited chatter of family members waiting for the choral program to begin.

Dan and Joe stood as the ladies took their seats. When they were settled, Joe leaned over to Dan. "Did you tell Beth how nice she looks?" he whispered as he flipped through the pages of his program.

"What are you, my mother?"

"You didn't, did you?" Joe shook his head. "I can only do so much, Dan. You're going to have to start picking up the slack."

The lights dimmed and Elsie leaned forward. "Shh, boys."

The evening began with introductions by the staff, and then each class performed a song for the audience. When they got to Amy's class the Gallagher family went crazy with applause and cheers.

Dan's whistles could be heard above the crowd. He couldn't help himself. *Proud* didn't begin to describe how he felt as Amy beamed from the stage, her little hands covering her mouth while she tried not to giggle. Finally, she shot a little wave in his direction.

His daughter.

Amy's music teacher, Mrs. Harlan, walked up to the microphone and spoke clearly, with perfect enunciation. "Could you please hold your applause until after the performance? Thank you."

A titter of laughter rippled across the auditorium and several of the Gallaghers' neighbors looked over at Dan.

"Think she's talking to us?" he whispered to Beth.

"No. I think she's talking to you." She laughed quietly.

"No? I…" He turned to her and paused. Tonight Beth's caramel hair was pulled back in a fancy updo, and tiny red stones glittered on her ears. There was something almost ethereal about her beauty in the dim glow of the aisle lights.

Dan forgot what he was about to say. Flustered, he turned his head to watch his daughter.

"You looked beautiful up there, Pumpkin," Dan said.

"Could you see my necklace?" Amy asked. She held up the silver chain with a tiny heart charm.

"Where did you get that, dear?" Elsie asked.

Amy grinned with pride. "Dr. Beth gave it to me."

"Oh, Beth, that necklace is simply lovely. How sweet of you," Elsie said.

Beth smiled, her cheeks pink at the praise. She turned to pull the tulip-shaped glass sundae dishes out of the cupboard for Elsie.

"Want some help with that?" Dan asked her.

"I've got them. Thanks."

"You're kind of amazing," he said, his voice low.

"Me?" she asked as she set the last two ice cream dishes on the counter.

"Yeah. How'd you know that was just the perfect thing to give Amy?"

"I pretended I was a little girl who had a mother who cared."

"Beth." The word whooshed from his lips as the painful truth of her words reached him.

She raised a brow.

"Like I said. You're amazing."

"Okay," Elsie said. "I have vanilla, chocolate and strawberry ice cream and chocolate, marshmallow and caramel topping." She glanced around. "Joe, can you grab the whipped cream can from the fridge? And Dan, the sprinkles and nuts in the cupboard, too, if you could get them, please?"

"GG, I want crushed Oreos on mine."

"Of course. You're the star. You can have whatever you want," Elsie said.

"Can't make a sundae without maraschino cherries," Dan said from where he leaned against the counter.

"Don't just stand there," Elsie called out. "They're in the refrigerator."

They took turns filling their sundae dishes with ice cream and toppings.

"Amy, careful with that whipped cream," Elsie said.

"Let me help you," Dan offered. He stood behind his daughter and placed his finger over hers as she sprayed the whipped cream. Glancing at Joe, Dan moved Amy's finger slightly to the right, until the can was positioned exactly to the perfect trajectory to douse his brother's hand with whipped cream.

Joe jumped back. "Hey, cut it out, Amy," he laughed.

Dan shot a wink to Beth and she smiled.

"Daddy did it," Amy said, unable to stop giggling.

"Uh-huh." Joe washed the cream off his hand. "Blame it on Daddy."

Amy kept giggling.

"What do you have there, Beth? Only vanilla with chocolate sauce?" Dan asked.

"I'm a woman of simple tastes," she said with a smile.

"Yeah, clearly you are. And to think I once thought you were high-maintenance," he said.

"I'm not that girl."

"One might mistake you for a country girl if one didn't know better," Dan said, his lips twitching.

"Fortunately, you know better," she returned, without revealing anything. Beth had an excellent poker face.

"Daddy, my certificate from the music program is gone." Amy lifted the tablecloth and looked underneath, then began to search the kitchen counters.

"Maybe you put it in your room," Elsie said.

"No, I didn't." Amy sniffed.

"No crying, Pumpkin. Take a deep breath," Dan said. "Let's have a plan here."

Amy did as he said and then looked up with watery eyes.

"Where did you see it last?" he asked.

"In the truck."

"Then I'll go look in the truck."

Beth placed her spoon in her empty dish. "You haven't finished your ice cream. I'm done. I'll go."

"We can both go," Dan said. He turned to Amy. "Put mine in the freezer for me, please?"

She nodded. "Thank you, Daddy."

"No problem. We have to have that certificate. I understand."

Beth and Dan donned their coats and walked across the yard to the garage. The snow had melted from the path and their steps were nearly silent. Tonight was much was warmer than it had been, and above them a full moon lit their way.

Beth paused for a moment to look at the sky. "My last night in Paradise," she mused.

"I'll grab a flashlight from the glove box and check the front seat," Dan said, "if you want to check the back."

"Sure."

The car made a familiar *ding-ding-ding* sound when he opened the door and turned on the dome light. Dan flipped back the mats and slid his hand beneath the seats. "Nothing."

"Look, here it is. Under the passenger seat. I can see the corner of the paper." Beth gave a ladylike grunt. "I think I can get my hand under there."

He came around to the passenger door and shone the light on the area. She slowly inched her hand into the small space. "Careful, don't hurt yourself," he said.

"I'm more concerned about that certificate," Beth said. "Oh, I can feel it now."

The only sound was the rustle of the crisp paper.

"Yes." She held it in the air and turned around, smack into him, her shoulder hitting his chest.

Straightening, he reached out to steady her with his hands. The certificate floated to the floor of the truck.

Beth licked her lips. "Um, I…"

Without thinking, Dan lowered his head until his mouth covered hers.

Her hands drifted and gripped his shoulders as he gently tunneled his fingers through her hair, cupping the back of her head in his hand.

Lost. Lost in the sweetness of Beth.

Moments passed and Dan finally moved enough to release her lips. Her head rested against his shoulder, the palm of her right hand beneath his coat, over his heart. With Beth tucked under his chin, he inhaled the flowery scent of her shampoo, mixed with a slight hint of chocolate and vanilla.

Why can't I hold her like this forever?

Finally, he stepped away, avoiding her gaze. "I, uh, I guess we'd better get that back to Amy." His voice was husky with emotion.

"Yes."

Dan felt chilled without her touch. He gently took her hand and held it as they walked up to the house.

"I'm not going to apologize, Beth, because that would be dishonest."

"You don't have to apologize."

"Do you ever wonder about…" He glanced at her and then focused on the house.

"What?"

"If things were different. If our lives had taken different paths?"

"No. I try not to think about what-ifs."

Beth was as guileless a person as he'd ever met. He looked at her chin, her heart-shaped face and her straight little nose. His gaze met hers. Those soft blue eyes. This was all he had to remember her. He'd remember every single thing about how she looked in this moment, beneath the pale yellow glow of the porch light, her lips swollen from his kisses.

Realization poleaxed him and he took a deep breath, unable to deny that he had fallen in love.

Dan reached out and slowly tucked a strand of Beth's shimmering hair back in place. Then he glanced away.

What did he have to offer her? Nothing. There was no way he could ask her to stay.

Chapter Thirteen

"I'll be back soon," Beth said. The words, like déjà vu, echoed in her ears. Hadn't she said nearly the exact same words one week ago? At the time, they'd been a thin platitude meant to placate her cousin. How things had changed. Now she couldn't be more sincere as she sat with Ben at Elsie's kitchen table on Saturday morning.

"Even though it's a small town?" he asked with a chuckle.

"Yes," she murmured. "Even though it's a small town."

Ben smiled.

"Crazy, huh?"

Her cousin shook his head. "No. Not crazy."

"I used to think you didn't get me," she said.

"Oh, Beth. I do. I remember what you were like when you came to live with us."

"Yes. I was mad at the world in those days."

"I think you were mad for a lot longer than that. Maybe even until recently. Not that you didn't have a good reason."

"No, Ben. I wasn't mad. I was ashamed."

"Ashamed?"

"Of my past, of not having someone who loved me."

"Oh, Beth. I'm so sorry."

"It's okay. I've figured out a lot while I was here in Paradise. I'm a different person than when I came. The truth is, I'm much nicer to myself because of this little detour. I've also discovered that my five-year plan was a five-year prison."

"Wow, it has been quite a week," he exclaimed.

"More than you can imagine."

He nodded. "You know Sara and I would like nothing better than to have you come and be a regular part of our lives. After all, you *are* family."

Family. For the first time in her life Beth was embracing the word. She was learning to understand that the emotions stirring inside her, while foreign, were normal. She had simply never experienced normal yearnings for hearth and home before.

"That position is still open at the hospital," Ben said. "Any chance…?"

Beth smiled at him. "I don't know what to tell you. My stuff has already been shipped to New York. I've given them my word. That's enough reason to go." She gave a wry smile. "I have to admit that I'm excited to see what's ahead."

"Okay, just remember that you managed fine for, what, eight days without your stuff."

She paused. "You know you're right. That's pretty amazing all by itself."

"The truth is, the job will still be here in a month," Ben said. "It will probably be here six weeks from now. In case you change your mind after you've finished your six week-long commitment." He grinned. "Sara and I have a running joke about trying to get doctors willing to work in rural areas. We can't figure out why they don't jump at the chance for a job with a noncompetitive salary, no perks, and a location smack-dab in the middle of Paradise."

Beth laughed. "I certainly gave you a hard time about the job when I arrived, didn't I?"

"No. Not much different than when I arrived in Paradise," Ben said. "I was here for a reason. I was running from God."

"What changed for you, Ben?" Beth asked.

"I stopped fighting the Lord. I gave it all up. Simple as that."

She shook her head. "Dan kept trying to tell me how simple it is. I don't mind letting God into my heart, but giving up control of my life? Not sure I can wrap my head around that."

"Surrender is the most difficult thing there is. Yet it's the only way. Control is a thankless god, Beth."

"I know you're right, and I'm working on it." She picked up her coffee cup.

"Good, because you deserve to be happy."

"Are you happy?" Beth asked.

"I am. Happier than I've been in my entire life. My wonderful wife and babies aside, I'm happy because I'm right where I'm supposed to be."

"The funny thing is that I think I could be happy here, too."

"Then why are you leaving?" Ben asked.

"I'm waiting for a better reason to stay."

"I hope you find that reason, because I have this gut instinct that Paradise is where you're supposed to be."

"I'll let you know what happens," she said with a solemn smile.

"Please do. Keep in touch. You have phones in the big city. No excuses."

Beth shook her head.

"I'd better get going." Ben stood. "I've got patients to see."

Standing, she embraced her cousin. "Thanks, Ben, and give Sara my best. Oh, and kiss those babies for me, will you?"

"Will do, and you think about what I said."

"Promise."

She waved to Ben as she watched him go, and then she headed back inside. The house was quiet. Joe had driven Elsie to her Saturday morning doctor appointment and they'd taken Amy with them. Dan would be by soon to drive Beth to the airport.

Amy had cried when she'd said goodbye. The hardest thing Beth had done in a long time was say goodbye to Amy Gallagher without crying herself. She'd fallen in love with the six-year-old long before she had fallen in love with the little girl's daddy.

Beth folded the last of her clothes that were in the dryer, and added them to the suitcase. This was probably the first trip she'd ever taken where she hadn't picked up a souvenir—well, except for the recipes Elsie had given her.

As she carefully checked the room to be certain she hadn't left anything, her glance landed on the Bible Elsie had offered her. Beth picked up the leather book and tucked it in the pocket of her suitcase.

After zipping up the sides, she rolled the case into the hall to the front door, propping her tote bag on top, careful not to smash the sandwiches and cookies Elsie had given her earlier this morning.

"You never know when you might be stranded," Elsie had said with a laugh.

Before this week, Beth would have laughed as well. Instead, she'd gratefully taken the brown bag.

She walked through the house one last time, memorizing everything. She stopped in the hallway and examined the photos of Dan, his sisters and

Joe. They were the usual school portraits taken from elementary school through awkward adolescence.

Usual to most people, but not to Beth. She had nothing like this to record her life. No photos, no mementos. The only thing she had was a mother who'd labeled her daughter a mistake.

Another reason why staying the course had been so important. Careful planning protected Beth from the pain of facing what was absent in her life. She had created a detailed road map for her life, but one stop in Paradise had changed everything. Now it was time to step away and reevaluate.

If only she could take Paradise with her in a blue Mason jar, like the one that held the game tiles Dan had offered her. There were so many things she'd bring with her if she could: the smell of the hay in the barn, the sound of the cows lowing and the exultation of seeing the birth of a calf. Moonlight over the ranch, highlighting a field full of snow angels. Elsie's cooking, and the warm smiles that welcomed her each day at the Gallagher kitchen table. Amy's joy as she learned the piano, and the mental snapshot Beth took of Amy in those silly red glasses, playing teacher.

The whisper-soft touch of Dan's lips on hers.

If only…

Beth sat down at the piano and lifted the fallboard. Her fingers drifted gently over the keys. She began to play the first little melody she had taught

Amy, repeating the song over and over again until her vision was blurry with moisture. Then, hands in her lap, she closed her eyes, bent her head and prayed.

"It's me again, Lord. Beth Rogers. You must be getting tired of me. I think Dan was right. I am lost. I don't want to be lost anymore. Please, show me what's next. I know that if I ask You enough times, eventually I'll hear Your voice."

"Sand dunes in the mountains?" Beth asked as Dan's truck passed yet another sign for the turnoff to the Great Sand Dunes National Park.

"Yeah. You've never heard of it? Home of the largest sand dune in North America. Star Dune is 750 feet tall."

"I'm embarrassed to say that I have not."

"I'll put that on the list of things to do when you come out for a visit."

She paused at his words, unsure if she should be encouraged or not. "What's the lure of sand dunes?" she finally asked.

"Tourists come from all over to ride the dunes. Walk up and slide down on sleds and boards."

"Okay," she answered, with another curious peek at him.

She'd never heard Dan so chatty. He'd barely allowed her to get a word in edgewise since they left the house thirty-eight minutes ago. Now, as the signs for the airport became more and more frequent, suddenly he was quiet.

They rode in silence and Beth struggled for the words she needed to say before she left him.

They finally burst out. "Dan, what if I didn't go?"

His head jerked around and the truck swerved. "What?"

"What if I stayed in Paradise?"

For a brief moment his eyes lit up and then he blinked and shook his head firmly. "No. Beth, you have to go to New York."

"Do I?"

"Yeah. You've got a great opportunity waiting for you."

"But what if I want to stay?"

The truck slowed as Dan turned to look at her. From behind them a car honked. "Maybe I'd better pull over."

He eased the car to the side of the highway and switched on his flashers. Still staring straight ahead, he swallowed, gathered his thoughts and then finally spoke. "Why? Why would you give up a job of a lifetime? Remember how many candidates you told me you beat out for this position? One hundred—wasn't that what you said? How long has it taken you to work your way up to this chance?"

"Years. And I know I said that, but sometimes people change. Sometimes their goals change," she said softly.

He stared straight out the window, his expression firm. "Not you. You said so."

"What else did I say?" she returned, irritation starting to lace her voice.

"I don't know, but I know you need to get on that plane. You need time and distance to reevaluate what you think you feel."

"What I *think* I feel?" Beth longed for the courage to tell him how she really felt.

"Yeah. Things may look different when you get some distance between you and Paradise."

"Dan, look at me," Beth said.

When he turned, his face was like stone, and only for a moment did she see something flash in his eyes when they locked with hers.

"You know this is real, Dan. As much as I do."

"It's only been a week, Beth. You have a life waiting for you."

"Why did you kiss me last night?" she whispered.

This time the pain was clearly evident on his face. "I'm sorry. I really am." He reached out to touch her fingers and she inched away. "Beth, I can't—"

She raised a hand. "No. Don't you dare." She knew what he was going to say. Dan Gallagher was rejecting her.

The reason hardly mattered anymore, because it wouldn't change anything.

He took a deep breath and wrapped his hands around the steering wheel. "Maybe we should have talked about this before now, but I wanted to pretend everything was going to work out somehow. I didn't sleep last night once I realized that I was fooling myself. We both know that we'd be crazy to think that this could work. I can't fit into your world and your future isn't here."

"People make adjustments all the time." *Was she pleading with him? No. She wasn't going to beg.*

"You shouldn't have to make adjustments," Dan said.

"This isn't only about me," Beth answered.

"You're right. It's about Amy, and Mom and even Joe. You can't come into their lives and then decide down the road that you don't like the fit."

Her head snapped back as though he'd struck her. "I think you're mistaking me for someone else."

His cell's alarm buzzed and he picked the phone up. "Your flight leaves soon. We need to go."

Dan eased the car back onto the highway.

Ironic that she'd worked so hard and long to ensure that she'd never be rejected, and here she was again, back where she'd started.

Unseeing, she looked out the passenger window. *This was much more painful than she remembered.*

Beth straightened her shoulders and swallowed the despair lodged in her throat. Yes, she was alone. But that was nothing new. She'd survived her mother leaving. She would survive this.

"Hey, look, we've got a curbside parking spot," Dan said as casually as if they had been discussing the weather minutes ago. He pulled over to the curb and jumped out, grabbing her suitcase from the back.

"Good luck, Beth."

She was well past stunned, and was already in regroup mode, putting on her "everything is fine" face. Beth smiled at him. "Thanks, Dan. For everything."

"I didn't do anything. You blessed our lives over and over. Thank you."

"Take care," she whispered.

"Yeah, sure. You, too."

"What was that verse you shared with me?"

He frowned, confused.

"Learn from your past. But don't live there." Beth nodded. "Yes. That's it," she murmured to herself. She took the handle of her suitcase and swiveled it around. *No looking back. No looking back.* If she repeated the words long enough, they might heal her broken heart.

Joe walked around the barn with a clipboard and a pen. "What time are you leaving to take Beth to the airport?" he asked Dan. "Think you can stop and pick up those vaccinations from the vet?"

Dan rested his arms over a stall fence. "I already took her to the airport."

Joe's head jerked up. "That was quick. Did you open the car door and dump her at the curb or what?"

"I dropped her off in front of the terminal. What's wrong with that?"

"Tell me you're kidding." Joe set the clipboard on the work counter with a thump and turned to look at his brother. "Come on, tell me that you parked the truck and walked her in and all. You did that, right?"

"No."

Joe gave a slow shake of his head. "So I'll wager you didn't talk to her. Tell her how you feel?"

"How do I feel, Joe?" Dan muttered, his temper simmering, hot and angry, below the surface.

"You tell me."

"Beth has a plane ticket to New York and the job of a lifetime waiting for her. I'm not going to be the guy who stands in her way."

"That wasn't the question." Joe met his gaze. "You know I've always respected you, Dan. You've always been a man who did the right thing. But you're way off the mark with this situation. Way off."

Dan raised his palms. "Come on, Joe. Say I do have feelings for her—so what? I've known her a week. *A week.* How can this possibly be real?"

"No guarantees, pal. Ever. Life doesn't work like that. But you can't stop taking chances because you don't want to risk getting hurt again."

"Seriously? Is that the best you can do?" Dan paced back and forth across the barn. "Do you think I haven't lain awake at night thinking this through? No matter how I look at things, it's a lose-lose proposition."

He was angry. He didn't know why but he was angrier than he had been in a long time. Even angrier and more confused than when Amy's mother had left.

All because he'd gone and fallen in love with Beth Rogers.

And that ticked him off. Royally. No, he didn't live in the past, but today it was clear that he hadn't learned anything from the past, either.

The absurdity of it all was that Beth had been upright and honest with him all along.

He'd heard her talking to Ben. She had plans. But had she planned on Dan falling in love with her? Not likely.

He slammed his closed fist against a rail.

"Now that's a smart move. Bang up your hands and you can't do anything."

"Back off, Joe."

"It's not too late. Call her. Tell her that you love her."

Dan's shoulders sagged in defeat. "What are you talking about?"

"Give her a chance to decide what she wants. Don't make the decision for her."

"No. There is no way I can do that to her. You don't know what she's been through. A lesser person would have never made it this far." Dan leaned over the rail and hung his head. He pulled his hat down and swiped at his eyes. It killed him to think of what Beth Rogers had suffered in life. No one deserved that, especially not her.

He took a ragged breath. "I'm not going to be the one who takes away everything she's worked her entire life for."

"Have you ever considered that she wants you to ask her to stay?"

"She'd only regret staying. Maybe not today or tomorrow, or a year from now even. But someday she'll look at me and the ranch, and Paradise, and wonder what she's doing here."

"I don't think you're right. I think Beth has been waiting her entire life for a home. Give her a chance."

"No can do." Dan turned away from his brother.

He rubbed his chest with his fist. The aching was almost physical. But no matter how much it hurt, he had to let Beth go. *Because* he loved her.

This was the right thing. For everyone.

Chapter Fourteen

Beth unbuttoned her coat as she walked down the street. Spring was in the air in New York. She glanced up at the blue, cloudless sky that peeked between the skyscrapers. Around her, the trees that lined Broadway had begun to bloom. She passed the Woolworth Building and stopped to admire the neo-Gothic exterior.

What would Paradise be like in the spring? All those wide-open spaces with the mountain peaks as a backdrop. So different from New York. Was it possible to be a city girl and a country girl?

The bigger question was what would be going on at the Gallagher Ranch? Cattle would be out to the farther pastures. She'd learned that much in her short time as a ranch hand. Dan had said that the next thing they would be doing was vaccination and branding. Joe would begin preparing his fields for hay seeding.

Here everything was straight up. There was no vast horizon with sunsets and sunrises that filled the line of sight for miles and miles. Beth could barely see the night sky from the little window next to her bed. The only green grass was in the small parks that dotted the city.

Her biggest frustration was that after being here a month she continued to find herself getting lost. There was no grounding yourself by the mountains. She was still trying to understand the boroughs, the subway system and the buses. Then there was uptown and downtown and midtown. East and west. Now, that was a puzzle. Beth tried to cut herself some slack and remember that natives had been doing this all their lives.

She had discovered a shop that sold cronuts, a hybrid croissant and doughnut, and she'd waited in line forty-five minutes for one. Good, though absolutely no comparison to the oatmeal cinnamon raisin cookies with lemon frosting from Patti Jo's Café.

Beth shook her head. Who'd have believed that a mere four weeks ago she'd been delivering calves on a ranch? Paradise was the biggest, most unexpected adventure of her life. But New York was the adventure she'd always planned for, and she was determined to make the most of it. For the first time in her locum tenens career she wasn't hiding in temporary housing during her assignment. No, she purposed to get out and meet the world. And she was enjoying the world.

The medical offices had closed this morning for a computer upgrade and Beth didn't have a patient until one. There was plenty of time to be a tourist without actually letting on that she was one.

All she had to do was walk the city walk, confident face forward, no eye contact, and certainly no smiling and greetings to strangers on the street, as in Colorado.

Her attention was caught by the bright and colorful wares of a shirt vendor, and she hurried her steps toward the curbside kiosk.

"Two for ten dollar," the vendor called. "Two for ten dollar."

Elsie was certainly worth two genuine, authentic knockoff sweatshirts. Beth giggled as she read them, imagining Elsie's reaction. She finally settled on Fun Size and I'm a Keeper.

"Two for ten dollar."

"Thanks. I'll take those two," she said, pointing to the blue one and the pink one.

As the vendor folded the sweatshirts, Beth had a mental imagine of Elsie breezing through the house in the shirts, with a kitchen towel draped over her shoulder and her silver-and-black curls bouncing with every move.

How she missed Elsie, and her cooking, too. Beth hadn't taken the time to try the recipes yet. But she would, she told herself. All part of the new Beth who did what she wanted, and not what she thought everyone else expected her to do.

When she was jostled from behind, Beth turned. A tall man in a leather jacket smiled at her. "I'm sorry," he said.

"Not a problem," Beth replied.

She watched him walk away. Handsome, but no Dan Gallagher. No one was as tall or as handsome as Dan, and certainly no man was as charming, or chivalrous. Dan rode horses and snowmobiles, and delivered babies and cows, and kissed her as if she was the most precious and delicious thing in the world.

He rejected you.

In her heart she had already forgiven him. Dan was afraid and she couldn't hate him for that. Beth understood fear only too well.

What would she do about the chasm that fear had dug between them? That was the real question. She continued to read the Bible she'd brought from Elsie's and offer up her simple prayers, believing that God would answer her. After all, it was Dan who'd told her to talk to God. His words had pretty much changed her life.

Looking up, she realized she was outside a church. The one she passed going to work each day. Wrought-iron gates with glass lanterns surrounded the perimeter. There was an oak statue inside the fence. Beth tilted her head back to see the stained-glass window. She followed the sidewalk to the entrance and stepped in through the open gates. The sign said that the chapel was currently open to the public.

As if welcoming the world, the front doors had been left open and the spring breeze glided through. Beth followed.

It had been too many years since she'd been inside a church. And what a church this was. The floors were marble inlaid tiles. Cut-glass chandeliers hung from the ceiling. An amazing window of small panes was the backdrop for the altar. Behind the pulpit a golden coronet stood, adorned with six golden feathers.

She slid into a pew and sat, silently absorbing the overwhelming peace and sanctity of the chapel, barely able to raise her eyes to enjoy the beauty.

This was what Dan was talking about. The grounding presence of a God who loved her unconditionally. Who first loved her and forgave her.

Maybe it was time for Beth to do the same.

She eased into a kneeling position and began to offer up a prayer of forgiveness for her mother.

It was time to let go of the past.

Beth entered the medical suite through the private staff door and went directly to her office. She reached for her white coat hanging behind the door just as the receptionist poked her head in.

"Dr. Rogers, there's a man here to see you."

"My one o'clock patient?"

"No, this isn't a patient. He says he's here from Colorado, and wanted to know if you could fit him in. Apparently he has a flight out in a few hours."

Beth's heart raced and she gripped the edge of the desk.

"Is he tall and dark?"

"Tall and dark, and very yummy." The receptionist giggled. "He's wearing cowboy boots, too."

Blood roared in Beth's ears as her heart kicked into overdrive. She feigned a calm she was far from feeling. "Is my first patient here?"

"No, he and his wife called, and they're running about fifteen minutes late. That means you have plenty of time for Mr. Hunk." The younger woman winked. "He's in the well-patient waiting area."

"Uh-huh. Thank you."

Beth touched a hand to her chignon and straightened her pink sweater and gray pencil skirt before pushing open the door. She recognized the tall build and those broad shoulders. He wore jeans and a nice gray-striped dress shirt. The sleeve of his right arm was pinned up.

Joe Gallagher.

"Joe?"

Joe turned and did a double take. "Wow. Look at

you." He walked around her. "You're even prettier than when you were in Colorado."

"Thank you. Glad I passed inspection. You look pretty good yourself."

"Okay to give you a hug?" he asked.

"Of course." Beth slid her arms around his shoulders and squeezed. "I've been taking hugging lessons since I arrived."

"What?"

"A silly joke." She waved a hand in dismissal.

"Do you have a minute?" he asked. "I'm sorry I didn't give you any notice."

"Sure. I have about fifteen minutes before my patient arrives. How long are you here?"

"In and out. I have a late-afternoon flight.

"That's too bad. I would have loved to show you around." She opened the door and Joe held it as they walked through. "My office is down here." The receptionist gave Beth a discreet thumbs-up as they passed by the front desk.

"Here. Have a seat," Beth said.

"Nice office."

He was right. It was a nice generic office. Tones of gray, with lots of brass fixtures. A rented pastoral painting graced the wall.

Joe walked over to the window. "That's got to be a very high-priced real estate view."

"I'm sure it is," Beth said with a smile.

"You're probably wondering who let me loose in the city," he said as he turned around.

"I was."

"This is a stopover. I'm headed to a reunion of my outfit from Afghanistan. We meet in D.C. tomorrow. Got bumped from my last flight and rerouted through New York."

"Long day then."

"Yeah, and you should have seen me trying to find this building. Cabbie didn't exactly speak fluent cowboy."

She laughed. "Cultural diversity strikes again."

"You said it, and I'm thinking I have to get out more." Joe smiled, the effect lighting up his face.

Joe Gallagher was handsome, smart, confident and stubborn. He would certainly be a handful for some woman when the day came for him to settle down.

Beth couldn't help a little chuckle. He was exactly like Dan.

"Something funny?" Joe asked.

"No, just thinking."

When he sat down across from her desk and crossed his legs, Beth sat down in her desk chair.

"So, how do you like it here?"

"Do you mean in here?" she said, her eyes sweeping the room. "Or out there?"

"All of the above."

"The practice is nice and the clientele pay their

bills, so I have no complaints. My hours are cushy. No hospital patients."

"Sounds sort of underwhelming for a gal that can deliver calves."

She laughed. "When you put it that way, I guess you're right."

"What about the city?"

"I can now ride the subway without getting lost, and I can walk down the street like a native."

"Well done." He raised his hand in the air and reached across the desk to give her a high five.

"What's the status on your prosthesis?" Beth asked.

"They've got me using a temporary one several hours a day for a couple months. Then I graduate to the myeoelectric one."

"Good news. Right?"

Joe nodded.

"Everything is okay, back home?" she asked.

"Things are great. Mom passed her stress test with an A plus. Her only homework is to keep exercising and eating right." He met Beth's gaze. "Everyone loved that care package you sent. Including me. Thank you."

"You're welcome."

"Actually," he continued, "no one knows I stopped by to see you. And I like to think maybe that rerouted plane was God's way of encouraging me to dabble in my brother's business."

Joe grinned. It was a crooked grin, a lot like Dan's. "Beth, my brother is crazy about you."

"You came all the way here to tell me that?" She stiffened and glanced away. "I don't think…"

"Please, hear me out."

"Sure, I'll give you a chance to plead his case. But you only have about ten minutes."

"I'd better talk fast then." Joe scooted to the edge of his seat. "Beth, Dan is a man who wouldn't want to disappoint anyone. He was trying to do the right thing by letting you go. Craziest thing I ever heard of, but it's the truth."

"The right thing. An easy way to say 'so long,' without any explanations, isn't it?"

"Let's not get off track here." Joe put up a palm. "And please don't shoot the messenger. I've got cows back home that need me."

She couldn't help smiling, which was exactly what he had intended.

"Dan refuses to stand between you and your plans, Beth."

"My plans were my protection, Joe. The constant striving for my goals kept me insulated so I didn't have to deal with reality. I needed to be saved from my plans." She sighed. "I realized that about the time I was packing my bags for the airport."

"Maybe you should tell Dan that."

"I tried, but he was so stubborn, so dead-set determined to get me on that plane…."

"Yeah, there is that Gallagher stubborn streak. Fortunately, it skipped me."

She chuckled and then paused. "You know this really isn't funny."

He rubbed his right arm. "I am aware, but for me, looking at the humorous side of things is the only way to keep from crying. Wouldn't you agree?"

"Ah, Joe, you Gallaghers are so charming. Too bad you can't bottle that charm. You'd make a fortune."

"Thanks. I think." He ran a hand through his hair. "There's something else you should know."

"Yes?"

"I want you to understand what's going on with Dan. He likes to pretend he was the wayward son who found his way, but that's not exactly what happened. He was asked to come home. Dad was dying. I was still in Afghanistan, trying to get discharged. Mom was falling apart. The sisters were helping as best they could, but Dan was needed." Joe met Beth's gaze. "It was at that low point in his life that his wife decided she couldn't handle small-town life, or marriage and motherhood, and refused to move to Paradise with him."

Beth's eyes widened.

"Dan thinks he's over the past, but he's not quite there yet. Deep down, he's afraid you'd suffocate in Paradise and leave him, as well."

"I'm here and he's there. How do I bridge that gap, Joe?"

"I don't know." He shook his head. "I hadn't gotten that far in my plan."

She released a small smile.

"I know I'm putting you on the spot...."

"No," Beth assured him. "You aren't. But I still don't know what to do."

"Do you love Dan?"

She nodded, her heart swelling.

"Well, then all you have to is find a way back to Paradise to convince a stubborn cowboy that you two deserve a chance."

"That's all, huh?"

"You know that old saying—attempt something big enough that failure is guaranteed unless God steps in."

"This definitely qualifies."

"I'll be praying, Beth."

"Thanks, Joe."

"Keep remembering those snickerdoodles. I see more of those memories in your future."

She bit her lip, silently laughing. "What is it with you Gallaghers? Whenever I'm around your family I spend most of my time trying not to bust a gut laughing."

"Go ahead and laugh, Beth."

She did and then she came around her desk and hugged him. "Thank you for coming, Joe."

After he'd left, Beth sat at her desk, staring out at the pedestrians crossing Broadway as the street-lights changed from green to yellow and then to red.

She closed her eyes. "The next move is Yours, Lord."

Tossing her coat and briefcase on the couch, Beth dug through her purse for her ringing cell phone.

"Hello?" She moved closer to the front window and the view of a brick wall. After a month she was convinced the building she lived in had been wrapped in lead. Cell signals were nearly impossible.

"Beth, it's Ben. You okay? You sound out of breath."

"I just got home from work."

"How are you doing?"

"Good. Very good."

"That's too bad."

She hadn't expected that. Her laughter rang out. "You've been in Paradise too long. You've developed that local sense of humor."

"Sadly, you're probably right. Last week I was caught telling a fishing joke," Ben said.

"I'm so sorry for you."

"Yeah, right. Well, the reason I called is to let you know that due to the lack of viable candidates for the clinic physician position, I've gone to the hospital board and requested an increase in the base salary.

Now, you understand you'd have to work one Saturday a month."

"Maybe we can negotiate. Ask them to throw in a husband and a couple of kids and I'll sign."

"Beth?"

She shook her head. "That was a joke, Ben. I picked up the local humor, too, you know."

"So you're interested?"

"I am."

"How interested?"

The line was silent.

"More interested than I was six weeks ago. Oh, and Joe Gallagher showed up at my office yesterday," Beth said.

"Joe? Really? He never said anything about stopping in New York."

"It was apparently an undercover operation."

"Oh?"

"Yes. He gave me some things to think about, and asked me to consider moving back to Paradise."

"And what *are* you thinking, Beth?"

"Well, I talked to God about the situation and told Him I'd need a job if I was going to move back to Paradise. And here you are calling."

"Are you accepting the job?" Ben asked.

"Yes, Ben."

"Sara! She said yes."

Beth could hear Sara screaming in the background and the painful sound of babies crying.

"Oh, she woke up the twins, she's so excited. I hope you weren't kidding."

"Absolutely serious. But listen, Ben. There really is one deal breaker for me."

"Okay…"

"I don't want you to tell anyone that I've accepted. Not until I have chance to take care of some loose ends."

"Loose ends, huh? What about your contract in New York?"

"I have a six-week approval period, and I'm right under it. Either party can change their mind without penalty."

"That's some kind of timing. And your place?"

Though he couldn't see her, Beth nodded in agreement. "My condo wasn't going to come open for another month. I've been staying in temporary housing."

"Whoa. This all has the earmarks of being a God thing," Ben said.

"A God thing?" Beth asked.

"You know, those situations when everything falls into place and you know that the good Lord must have had His hand on things."

"Yes, then definitely, a God thing." She stared out the window, thinking about the phrase.

"I'm glad, Beth."

"Me, too." Her phone buzzed. "Oh, I've got Elsie on the other line now."

"No problem. Text me a number to fax the contracts when you have time."

"I will, and, Ben, thank you, for not giving up on me. And remember. Don't tell anyone."

Beth pressed the incoming call button.

"Guess who? It's Elsie."

"Elsie. Is everything all right?"

"Now you sound like me. I do that to my daughters when they phone." Her laughter trilled in Beth's ear. "I'm fine. I had a stress test last week and everything looks good."

"That's wonderful news." Beth wasn't going to let her know she'd seen Joe and heard the same news from him.

"Yes, and my daughter Leah is pregnant again. Twins. They run in the family."

"Oh, congratulations."

"We got your package. I had to call and thank you. You shouldn't have. But I'm glad you did."

Beth smiled.

"Love the sweatshirts. You sure know me, don't you?"

"I was walking down the street and they called your name."

"Ha. I can believe that. Oh, and Dan must love those caramels you sent, 'cause he won't share them with anyone."

Beth laughed.

"How are you doing in New York?"

"Things are going well, Elsie."

"Well, huh? Does that mean you like it there?"

"It means that I'm adjusting."

Elsie clucked her tongue. "Done any cooking?"

"I'm in temporary housing right now, so the kitchen is very tiny. But I have thought about making the chili, twice, and I also thought about making the tortilla soup a few times."

Elsie laughed. "Maybe I'd better send you a few more to think about. I have your address from your package."

"That would be great." Beth stopped. "Wait. No. I forgot that I'll be moving into another place soon. I'll let you know when I have a settled address."

"That'll be fine."

She heard the piano in the background. "Is that Amy?"

"Yes. She wanted you to hear her play."

"She sounds wonderful. May I talk to her?" Beth asked.

"Of course. She'll be so excited to hear from you. Let me get her."

Moments later Amy Gallagher spoke into the phone, her voice breathless with excitement. "Dr. Beth. Thank you for the ballet movie. I play it every day."

"Oh, I'm so glad."

"When are you coming back?"

"I don't know."

Amy sniffed. "I miss you so much."

"Oh, honey, I miss you, too."

Amy released another dramatic sniffle into the phone and then began to cry.

"Oh, boy." Elsie got back on the phone.

Beth grabbed a tissue and wiped her own eyes. "I'm sorry. I didn't mean to make her cry."

"No, it's not your fault. She misses you something fierce, Beth. We all do."

"I feel the same way, Elsie."

"Woof! Woof!"

"Is that Millie?"

"She can hear your voice."

"Oh, hug her for me. I can hear her jumping up and down." Beth paused. "So, um, how are your sons?"

"Dan's had an attitude since you left. We cut him a wide berth. But it's his own fault. And that Emily's been popping up here and there."

"Emily?"

"You know. The midwife." Elsie's voice became agitated. "I can't figure why some folks can't see what's right in front of their eyes."

"Weather's good?" Beth interrupted.

"Oh, beautiful. Spring in the mountains. About the prettiest time of year."

"I bet."

"Did I tell you that Joe's on a trip to D.C.?"

Beth could picture Elsie in one of her sweatshirts,

standing in the kitchen and looking out at the pasture as she chatted on the phone.

"Sounds like fun, though I'm sure the cows miss him. Speaking of which, whatever happened to that abandoned calf?" Beth asked.

"Joe bonded it with a momma who lost her baby. That calf is thriving like you wouldn't believe. All it takes is a little bit of love. Doesn't really matter who your momma is."

Beth stilled at the words.

Elsie's voice became soft. "Sure miss you, Beth. Did I tell you that already?"

"Yes. But that's okay." Beth ached with longing for Dan's mother and the rest of the Gallaghers.

"Are they keeping you busy at that new job?"

"Oh, yes. I love the job."

"Good. Good. Important to like what you're doing. Made any friends yet?"

Beth shrugged. "Not really. But you know, it's a big city and it takes a while."

"Not like Paradise, where everyone knows your name *and your business.*"

"That's exactly right."

"Remember you can always come home, Beth."

Home. Beth savored the word.

"Thank you, Elsie."

Chapter Fifteen

New York to Denver, and Denver to Alamosa. Welcome to the San Luis Valley Regional Airport.

Home sweet home.

Beth took a long swig of water as she waited for her bags at the carousel. Car rental next. A couple times she had toyed with the idea of letting Elsie pick her up, but the odds of Dan's mother keeping a secret weren't very good. Besides, Beth would need a car until she was settled in and had time to purchase one. She was determined to be in the driver's seat of her life from now on. Renting a car was a good place to start.

She stepped out into the Colorado sunshine and tried to take a deep breath. Too bad she couldn't get an oxygen transfusion. She'd already forgotten how thin the air was here.

Though she was tired, there was still a lot to do, and taking the red-eye out of New York meant she now had the entire day ahead of her.

The next step was to get a dog. All her life she'd wanted a dog, but had talked herself out of the idea, again and again. After all, she traveled, and a dog needed attention that she couldn't provide with her hours. Then there was that little voice that insinuated she might not be a good owner.

But Dan's dog, Millie, and Joe's border collies liked her.

The little cabin Ben had rented to her was located on the outskirts of Paradise, off the beaten trail. Lots of grass and trees. Perfect for a dog.

Beth drove straight to the San Luis Valley Animal Rescue, a no-kill shelter, for her scheduled appointment. She had already filled out the paperwork, and sent her references by email. While she could have found a dog online, she'd always hated blind dates. Why subject an animal to that?

The moment she walked into the bright yellow, indoor kennel she heard him. The loudest yapper in the place.

Then she saw him.

A lot of noise for such a little pup. He had confidence. Beth liked that. The exuberant little border collie mix was mostly black with a white patch on his face. *Patches.*

Beth Rogers became a bona fide dog owner.

It didn't take very long for her to wrestle the kennel into the backseat of the car and secure it with the seat belt. Patches barked before he finally settled into his kennel and fell asleep. She pointed the vehicle in the direction of Paradise and her new home.

This was the same rustic little cabin where Ben had lived before he and Sara married. Ben had liked it so much that he'd bought the place.

The cool mountain air blew through the windows of the rental car as Beth headed to her new home. Twice she pulled off the road into a rest stop simply to take in the breathtaking spring flowers that were beginning to bloom along the road, in the fields and at the base of the mountains. Forty-five minutes later, she pulled up to the gravel drive in front of the cabin.

She stood in the front yard simply soaking it all in. The cabin was nestled between tall conifers, and the unobstructed skyline stretched as far as she could see. The Colorado sky was bluer than blue and dotted with clouds. May in Paradise and a pleasant seventy-seven degrees. Perfection.

Turning her gaze to her new home, she was more than surprised. It was like a picture from a decorating magazine. A porch extended along the entire front of the cabin, and sported coral-red Adirondack chairs and aluminum tubs that overflowed with freshly planted geraniums.

Home.

Her home.

Beth looked skyward. "Thank You, Lord."

Patches urged her up the wooden steps, tugging

at his leash as though he knew this was his new home, as well. Laughing, she followed, found the key under the mat and opened the door.

The main living area had two oversize, dark brown leather chairs and a matching love seat arranged around a rough-hewn white cedar coffee table. A large Southwestern rug, in tones of brown and pottery red, with a thick fringe, covered most of the floor.

The kitchen, while small, had brown granite countertops and an island with two leather stools. Gleaming stainless steel appliances had been fitted into the area.

Rustic? That was obviously an inside joke, because the so-called "rustic" cabin was anything but. Not unlike Abel and Karen's cabin, where Beth had witnessed her first home delivery. Was that only a little more than six weeks ago?

The boxes she'd shipped to Ben's house were already here and waiting against a far wall. Patches sniffed around with excited approval. She agreed with the dog's assessment.

Beth opened the large stainless steel refrigerator. It was stocked with fresh essentials. Sara's doing, no doubt. She peeked out the window over the sink at the neatly mowed yard. A barbecue grill, outdoor furniture and a hammock decorated the area closest to the house. The grass stretched to a row of conifers and aspens, and on the right, dense woodland sheltered the property.

"Come on, little guy. Let's get us both a cold drink, and then I'll let you stretch your legs in that huge yard."

An hour later she called Ben.

"You made it," he said. Beth could hear the smile in his voice.

"I did, but I have a problem."

"Already? Are you okay?"

"Poison ivy."

"You went in the woods."

"I was chasing Patches," Beth said.

"Who's Patches?"

"My dog."

"You have a dog?"

"I do." She smiled as Patches settled on the rug in front of the not-so-rustic river stone fireplace.

"Good for you." He chuckled. "Are you sure it's poison ivy?" Ben asked.

"Oh, it's poison ivy. I spotted the plant after the fact."

"Where and what kind of reaction?"

Beth glanced down at her right leg, below her capri pants, where raised blisters were already appearing. "Both of my legs, and it sort of looks like they exploded with welts."

"Oh, man, that's too bad."

"Do you mind calling in a script for an oral corticosteroid, just in case? I have a history of reacting pretty badly to poison ivy and I start the new job soon."

"No problem. It goes without saying. Don't scratch. Keep the area clean and don't let it get infected."

"Yes, Doctor."

"Other than the poison ivy, how are you settling in?" Ben asked.

"I love the cabin. Although I'm thinking that it's a bit less rustic than you let on."

"Sara's fault. She completely redid the place. It's our escape."

"It's beautiful. Tell Sara that, and tell her thank-you for stocking the fridge." Beth ran a hand over the sparkling granite countertops. "Okay to use the infamous espresso machine?" She glanced over at the shiny black and stainless steel machine.

"Infamous?"

"Yes. I've heard several retellings of how Dr. Ben came to Paradise with only the clothes on his back and an espresso machine. I thought they were exaggerating."

"Sadly, it's true. Sort of had my priorities mixed up in those days," he admitted.

She laughed.

"Use anything you want," Ben continued. "Don't forget that Sara expects you for family dinner next Sunday, and then the following Monday is orientation at the clinic. Glad you came early to get settled in."

"Me, too, and don't worry, I have everything on my calendar." Beth grinned, barely holding back her excitement. Family dinner.

"Oh, and I just faxed that script over to the pharmacy. Let me know if you need anything else."

"Which pharmacy?"

"Paradise Pharmacy. The only pharmacy in town."

"Thanks." She put her phone down. Suddenly realization hit. *The only pharmacy in town?*

Beth had hoped to see Dan later, instead of sooner. Maybe she'd pick up the script today and maybe she wouldn't. But she was longing for oatmeal cinnamon raisin cookies with lemon icing, so now was as good a time as any to take a ride into town. Patches followed her as she grabbed her tote bag and headed into the bathroom to shower.

A glance in the steamy mirror affirmed that she did indeed look as if she'd been flying cross-country all night. Not much she could do about that. She washed her face and applied concealer to the dark circles under her eyes, then dried her hair and pulled it back into a low ponytail.

Beth looked down at the little dog who was sniffing the claw-foot bathtub and pedestal sink. "What do you think, Patches? Are we ready to brave Paradise?"

* * *

"Ben, this is Dan Gallagher over at the Paradise Pharmacy. Can you call me back?" He put down the receiver and stared at the script in his hand. Surely this was a mistake. When he'd pulled the fax off the machine, he'd stood there, stunned, as he read the patient's name. *Elizabeth Rogers.*

A mental image of the woman who had filled his thoughts appeared. The same images that kept him up night after night since she'd left. Beth's hair tumbling around her face, her lips full and pink after they'd shared a kiss. Her heart in her eyes as she gazed up at him. That picture was immediately replaced by her stoic expression as she'd tried to hide her pain when he'd dropped her off at the airport.

Dan grimaced. He was the one who had crushed the hope she'd offered. Time and again he had reviewed their last conversation. Her words echoed in his head.

"What if I stayed in Paradise?"

No way had he expected that or believed she meant those words.

Six weeks and he'd finally had the guts to face the truth.

He'd been a fool. A fool who was scared to death of what Beth offered. Terrified that she'd change her mind and break his heart by leaving. She did leave—and she did break his heart. But it was no one's fault but his own.

The pharmacy phone rang and Dan reached for the receiver. "Paradise Pharmacy, Gallagher here."

"Dan, this is Ben."

"Yeah, hey, sorry to bother you, but I was checking on this corticosteroid script."

"Can't read my chicken scratch?" Ben chuckled.

"No. I've learned to decipher your handwriting by now. It's your wife who gives me fits. But the name on the Rx? *Elizabeth Rogers?*"

Ben was silent.

"Ben?" Dan prodded.

"Yeah, that's correct, Dan. Elizabeth Rogers."

"Your cousin."

"Right."

The air whooshed from Dan's lungs and he grabbed the counter. Beth Rogers was back in Paradise and she hadn't told him. *Could he blame her?* a voice shot back at him.

"Beth is visiting you?" he finally asked, his voice raw.

"Not exactly."

Dan took a deep breath. "Not exactly?"

"Look, Dan, I sort of promised that I would keep my mouth shut." Ben cleared his throat. "But, ah, you know, now that I think about it, maybe I didn't give you all the information you need for that script."

"What?"

"Birth date. Allergies. *The patient's address and phone number.* You probably need that to get her insurance information. Who knows, you might have to deliver that script if she doesn't happen to make it by before you close. As her physician, I can tell you that she needs that prescription."

Suddenly, Dan grinned. "Right. Oh, yeah. Absolutely. I am on it." He fumbled with the pen in his hand. Grabbing a blank piece of paper, he began to write down the information as Ben gave it to him.

When he was done scribbling, Dan shook his head. "Thanks, Ben. I owe you, big-time."

"Yeah, you do. So don't disappoint me."

"No. No, I won't."

He glanced at the information. Beth was staying at Ben's cabin on the other side of Paradise. He knew the place—it was where Sara and Ben had held their engagement party. Dan wrote her birthdate on the script. Beth had a birthday coming up. There was so much he still didn't know about the woman he loved. But he intended to remedy that, really soon.

Dan glanced at the clock. Almost noon. He got off at three. Then he remembered that he'd promised to meet with Emily after work to go over the details for the free-clinic day the hospital was offering next month. He'd already canceled on her once.

Okay. Fine. He'd meet with Emily and then he'd head out to the cabin.

He picked up the receiver again and punched in Joe's cell number.

"Hear those cows?" his brother answered.

"Most people say hello when you call them," Dan said.

"I'm not most people. Those cows want fresh water."

"Look, I don't care about the cows. This is important."

"It had better be. Hang on a second, let me get out of the middle of the pasture," Joe muttered. He was back a moment later. "What's your emergency?"

"Beth is back."

"Visiting?" Joe didn't sound surprised.

"I don't know. Did you know she was here?"

"News to me."

"Any idea how I can fix things?"

"I told you what to do six weeks ago. Why do you keep asking me questions if you aren't going to listen to what I have to say?"

"I still love her," Dan murmured, more to himself than anyone else. He paced back and forth and then stopped.

"Of course, you realize that you're telling the wrong person." Joe's words were flat.

Dan ran a hand through his hair. "She's back. Doesn't that prove something?"

"Prove? You're missing the point here, Dan. Beth doesn't have to prove anything. You're the one who has to prove something. You may love her, but you don't trust her with your family. With your heart."

"You're supposed to be my brother. A little support would not be out of order here."

"I've got nothing for you," Joe said.

"Thanks," Dan muttered. "You've been a big help."

"You know what you have to do. There's no way to make crow taste good." Joe paused. "You just have to grab a fork and start eating."

"Any other sage advice?"

"You messed up once. Don't mess up again."

"Thanks."

"Look, Dan, it's going to all work out."

"How come you're so sure?"

"Because I've gone behind your back, and started praying for you."

"Thanks. I guess you're not such a lousy brother, after all."

"Don't start going all mushy on me."

Dan only laughed.

Right now he'd agree to take care of Joe's cows for a month if it meant a second chance with Beth. The fact was, he didn't have a clue what his next step was going to be, which generally meant he'd better start praying. Hard.

Beth parked the rental car at the far end of Main Street and attached Patches's leash to his collar before she got out. When her pant legs accidently rubbed against the blisters, shooting pain straight up her calves, she winced.

She could see the crisp awning of the café from her car. After plugging the meter with quarters, she and Patches started down the street.

What a difference in the downtown area now that spring had come to the valley. Planters dotted the sidewalks. The newly flowering plants and dark potting soil indicated that they had been recently planted.

An almost giddy excitement bubbled up inside her as she approached Patti Jo's Café and Bakery. This was where she'd realized she was in love with Daniel Gallagher. No matter what had happened since, this was one memory she would cling to for the rest of her life.

She stared through the window at the shop and shook her head. What had she been thinking? *Patches*. Some dog owner she was. Her dog couldn't go in and she wasn't going to leave him outside.

The door opened and a tall woman with a white bun anchored on top of her head nearly mowed Beth down. She backed up in surprise and straightened her pink slacks and crisp white blouse.

"You can't stand there or you'll be run over." She put her hands on her hips.

"I'm sorry," Beth murmured.

"Are you coming or going?"

"I wanted to get some cookies, but I don't want to leave my dog outside."

"Hand me the leash."

Beth turned it over to her at the command.

"Don't I know you?" The woman peered down at Beth.

"I don't think so."

"Dr. Elizabeth Rogers. You were snowed in at Elsie's place." She nodded knowingly. "Bitsy Harmony. I don't think we've officially met." Bitsy struck out her hand and took Beth's in a hearty handshake.

"Oh, yes. The Paradise Ladies Auxiliary," Beth said.

"Correct." Once again she looked Beth up and down, her sharp blue eyes missing nothing. "Does Elsie know you're in town?"

Beth's own eyes widened. She opened her mouth, then closed it, finally finding words. "Will you excuse me just a minute? I'll grab those cookies."

She pulled open the door to the café and moved quickly to the counter.

"Two oatmeal cinnamon raisin cookies, please. Oh, and maybe a couple carrot cake muffins. To go." Beth pulled out a bill and handed it to the cashier. "Thanks. Keep the change."

When she opened the door to the sidewalk, she found Bitsy kneeling beside Patches, stroking the pup behind the ears.

"Nice dog."

"Thank you, and thank you for watching him."
Bitsy stood.

"I'll be calling Elsie today," Beth said, "so I hope
you'll keep my secret. I'd like to surprise her."

"Does Dan know you're here?" Bitsy narrowed
her gaze.

"Dan?" Beth's eyes rounded.

"Well, sure enough, everyone knows what a don-
key he was to let you go." Bitsy shook her head.
"Men."

"I…" Beth was speechless.

"Oh, no worries," she said with a quick wink.
"It'll be our little secret. You take care now."

Beth stared as Bitsy strode down the street. The
woman was a locomotive.

"Come on, Patches. Let's put these goodies in
the car."

Beth sat in the car, thinking, as Patches stared
out the passenger window. Maybe this wasn't such
a good idea. There was no telling who else she'd run
into. She'd hoped to ease into her new life.

When a car door slammed, she looked up. Down
the street the glass door of the Paradise Pharmacy
opened and Dan Gallagher stepped out to the curb.
He glanced at his watch and looked down the street.

Unable to move, unable to think, Beth took in
every bit of his profile, savoring the image. The real
Dan was much better than her daydreams. And she

had dreamed of him long enough to know. As if he sensed that she was watching him, he narrowed his eyes and scanned up and down the street, a puzzled expression on his face. Then he turned around.

Beth turned in her seat. Emily Robbs crossed at the intersection and called out Dan's name. He responded with a smile and a wave.

A wave of despair slammed into Beth. She was too late.

Deep breath.

Coming to Paradise wasn't about the man. It was about walking the path God had prepared for her. Of course, she'd have to repeat that a couple hundred more times to convince her heart.

Beth encouraged Patches into the kennel, put the key in the ignition and headed home.

"This is a shoe and this is a chew toy. We'll work on recognizing the difference."

Dan laughed through the screen door.

Beth whirled around and her cheeks heated. Their gazes locked. She tried for nonchalance as she dropped the props in her hands. "I was talking to the dog," she finally said.

He kept laughing. "Yeah, I figured. But you should see how funny it looks from this side of the screen."

"What are you doing here?" She glanced at the

wall clock. Nearly six. Had his date with Emily ended early?

And why was she so annoyed? He'd caught her off guard. That was why. Without a chance to mentally prepare for this moment. Besides, she was wearing her oldest capris and a faded pink T-shirt. And she was barefoot, with her hair in a messy ponytail.

"Hey, Beth," he murmured, his voice gliding over her like velvet. "Good to see you."

"How did you know I was here?"

"Information on your script." He held up a white bag.

She glanced at him quickly through the screen. "Isn't that a violation of HIPAA or something?"

"I'm a pharmacist. Technically, you're my patient."

"Ben ratted me out."

Dan only shrugged.

Beth slid her feet into her sandals and inched closer to the screen. "Do you smell something?"

"Your dog?" he offered.

"My dog doesn't smell like pepperoni pizza."

He cleared his throat. "Think I could come in?"

"Fine." She opened the screen.

Undeterred by her attitude, Dan turned around and backed through the doorway.

"What are you doing?" she asked.

"Balancing act."

When he turned around, she saw the two pizza boxes in his arms.

"It *is* pizza." She looked at him. "You know, of course, that you can't make everything in life right by bringing a couple boxes of pizza, right?"

Dan's clear gray eyes sparkled. "This is the pre-apology warm-up."

Leave it to Dan to skip straight to the elephant in the room.

"Did you bring enough for all three of us?" she asked.

"Yeah, unless your dog eats more than his share. But I could always go for more."

"That won't be necessary." She stooped down to rub Patches on the head, but he eluded her fingers and immediately raced over to Dan.

"Nice dog," he said.

"He is. Be careful, the shelter told me he can be a little iffy around men."

Dan crouched down and held out his hand. Patches sniffed and then nuzzled his head into Dan's palm, begging to be petted.

"Or not," Beth said.

"We have a lot in common, me and…"

"Patches," she said. She went to the cupboard and pulled out dishes. "You both snore?"

Dan laughed. "You've changed, Beth."

"You mean because I made a funny?"

"No. But I like that. It suits you."

Her lips twitched as she pulled glasses from the cupboard and a pitcher of tea from the refrigerator.

"So what is it that Patches and you have in common?" she asked.

"You have our hearts."

"Dan." She met his gaze and sighed. "Pizza and the full-court press Gallagher charm. You must be desperate."

"Trust me. I am. Six weeks' worth of desperate."

"Have a seat," she finally said, offering him a stool at the granite island.

He settled himself across from her.

"Mind if we pray?" Beth asked.

"See? You have changed."

"I have you to thank for that." She hesitated for a moment and then took his hand. It was warm and strong in hers. It required all her concentration to focus on the prayer. "Lord, thank You for all You have given me. Bless this food to our bodies. Amen."

"Amen."

Beth quickly slid her hand from Dan's and reached for the pizza box at the same time he did. Their fingers collided and heat rushed into her face.

She was acting like a...

Like a woman in love.

"Go ahead," she said, her eyes on the box.

"Ladies first."

Beth served herself and then poured the tea.

"Thank you for the pizza. I was debating whether I should open a can of soup or open a can of soup for dinner."

He chuckled. "Some things don't change, I see. And you're welcome." He glanced around. "Nice place."

"I like it. It's good to finally put down roots."

His brows rose and surprise flickered in his eyes. "You're staying?"

"Yes. Is that so hard to believe?"

"No. Makes my job a whole lot easier."

Beth cocked her head. "Excuse me?"

"I'm here to beg you to stay." His expression was sincere.

Flustered, Beth froze with the pizza halfway to her mouth. "I, uh, I took a position at the Paradise Clinic."

"If you end up taking calls for the snowmobile team, you'll be my boss."

"I hadn't considered that." Appetite waning, she dropped the pizza and reached for her napkin while searching for a safer topic. "What about you? What have you been up to?" she asked.

Dan chewed a bite of pizza and swallowed. "Same old. Pharmacy forty hours a week, and rescue training once a month."

"I talked to your mom a few weeks ago."

His head jerked back. "My mom knew you were coming back here?"

Again, they were skirting around the real issue at hand. "No, Dan," Beth murmured. "Only Ben and Sara knew."

He nodded, digesting her information.

"May is beautiful in Paradise," she said as she stared out the window.

"The big Founder's Day celebration is coming up," Dan said.

"I guess you and Emily will be going."

"No." Dan sucked in a breath. *"I would never encourage her when I..."* He met Beth's gaze, pain and confusion in his eyes. "No."

"I'm sorry. I assumed." She shrugged. "Emily likes you and she's pretty much everything you need."

Silence stretched.

Patches whined and Beth picked up his chew toy and tossed it across the room.

"Beth, what I need is you."

She thought she'd imagined the husky, whispered words, but when her eyes locked with his there was nothing but honesty on his face.

"I have to know what's different, Dan." She swallowed, willing the emotion back. "You practically tossed me on that plane in April."

"I didn't trust you to love me, Beth. I was wrong." He looked away and then met her eyes again. "I'm so sorry."

Beth released the breath she'd been holding. He'd figured it out all by himself.

"You're right," she said. "We were thrown together for a week, and that week snowballed with emotions neither of us were prepared for or knew how to handle."

He nodded. "That's not an excuse for what I did," he said.

"I know." She paused. "My life began the day I met you, Dan. You showed me what I was missing, and how to laugh at myself." She smiled. "And you shared your God with me."

"That's the best thing I've heard since you left."

"For me it only gets better. I've forgiven my past and I've stopped planning for my future. I'm going to live my life today."

"Where does that leave us?" Dan reached across the counter and covered her hand with his.

"I love you, Dan."

He sucked in a breath, and the look in his eyes matched what was in her heart.

"I love you," she repeated with a smile. "That won't ever change. I'm here to stay, because Paradise is where I belong. It's what I *choose*. And I *choose* you, too. Forever."

Dan sat very still. "Beth, I love you. I'm so grateful for a second chance."

She moved around the island to stand in front of

him, this time allowing herself the luxury of running a hand through his hair.

"This is isn't about second chances, Dan. It's about not allowing fear to steal any more of our life. Our lives. Together."

He smiled and gently tucked a loose strand of hair behind her ear.

She shivered at his touch.

"Where do we go from here?" Beth asked.

"Maybe we can just take some time to enjoy each other and Paradise," Dan said.

"I'd like that," she answered.

"Me, too."

His hand circled her waist and she could feel his warm breath moments before he touched his lips to hers. She loved this man so very much.

He released her and put his forehead against hers, as he stared into her eyes.

"God is so good," Beth said with a smile.

"Amen," Dan said.

She laughed softly. "I can't wait to see your family."

He kissed the tip of her nose. "Welcome back to Paradise, Beth."

"It's good to be home," she murmured.

Epilogue

Elsie Gallagher patted Joe's arm as he escorted to her to a seat in the first pew of the Paradise Chapel, before he went to join Dan at the altar.

"Beautiful dress, Elsie," Bitsy Harmony commented from behind her.

Elsie glanced at her taupe silk dress with the pretty brocade jacket, and adjusted her corsage of white roses before turning in her seat. "Thank you. I have a Mother of the Groom sweatshirt adorned with tiny seed pearls, but Dan wouldn't let me wear it."

Dan winked at his mother from his position at the altar.

"Oh, look," Elsie said. "The doors are opening."

Dan cleared his throat and put on a smile.

"Nervous?" Joe asked.

"Yeah, I guess I am," Dan admitted. "Maybe she'll change her mind."

"Not a chance. She loves you."

"It was touch and go for a while there," Dan said. He adjusted his rose boutonniere.

"Only in your mind, Danny."

They stood silently as the rest of the guests were seated.

"I don't deserve her."

"True, but let's not dwell on that," Joe said.

Dan laughed. Good old Joe, he did know how to lighten the mood.

"Now, try to think positive," his brother added. "You're number three. In approximately five minutes you'll be married. That means Mom will be focused on me for a while."

"Yeah, that helps. Thanks." Dan grinned.

The processional started and Amy began to walk slowly down the aisle of the small church, exactly the way they had practiced at the rehearsal.

Her smile was radiant. Amy looked so grown-up in a pale apricot dress, with her dark hair long and shining. She was, after all, seven years old now.

Next was the matron of honor. Sara Rogers's dress was also apricot, a sheath, he'd been informed. She walked down the aisle on her husband's arm, smiling. Sara and Ben were more than pleased that Beth would be living in Paradise. They wanted the godmother of their babies close by.

Dan's dark-haired twin sisters, Rachel and Leah, followed, on the arms of their husbands.

They were easy to tell apart. Leah was the one who looked as if she was about to deliver. Possibly during the wedding. Dan's medical tackle box was stashed behind the pulpit just in case. He had to give his sister credit. She waddled nicely to the strains of the organ.

The music changed, signaling the imminent arrival of the bride. Dan took a deep breath in eager anticipation.

Beth was all in white, her hand gently resting on the arm of her uncle, Dr. Benjamin Rogers, Senior. Ben's father had flown in with his wife for the occasion. She wore some sort of sleek shimmering dress, her shoulders bare. Simple and elegant, like his bride.

Instead of wearing a veil, Beth had her hair pulled up and anchored with tiny apricot rosebuds. A single strand of pearls adorned her neck, and pearls decorated her ears. She carried a bouquet of peach and apricot roses and white peonies as she moved gracefully down the aisle.

Elizabeth Rogers, his love, his bride, and very soon, his wife.

When their eyes locked and her lips curved into a serene smile, Dan's breath caught in his chest.

"Not going to need CPR, are you?" Joe whispered.

"No, I'm good," he answered as Beth's steps drew her closer and closer.

As Dr. Rogers left the bride with her groom and took his seat, Amy exclaimed, "Look, it's snowing."

Heads turned to peer out the large windows on either side of the pews, and a hush fell over the congregation as the fat flakes danced in the autumn air.

A mere six months ago snowflakes just like those had brought Beth to him. Dan would be eternally grateful.

"Snow in September?" Beth was wide-eyed. "It's too early for snow."

"This is Paradise," Dan said.

"Maybe it's good luck," she whispered.

"No, I don't believe in luck. Those flakes are God's blessing on us."

Moisture filled Beth's eyes and she nodded in agreement. She leaned close and whispered in his ear, "There's no place I'd rather be than with the man I love, in Paradise."

* * * * *

Dear Reader,

Welcome back to Paradise.

As a registered nurse, working in the medical field, I learned early on that those called to this ministry profession are caregivers. They give generously and unconditionally, but often they have a difficult time receiving, and accepting a thank-you. That's because what they do is truly what they know they are called to do, and medical professionals don't do their jobs expecting thanks.

The same is true for Beth and Dan. I hope you enjoyed their story. I was especially endeared to this couple because I enjoyed them as people. They're caregivers with trust issues. Together they learn to trust God and trust each other.

I also completely fell in love with the Gallagher family. I hope to write more stories that feature these quirky characters who kept trying to hijack this book.

Drop me a line and let me know what you think. I can be reached at tina@tinaradcliffe.com or through my website at www.tinaradcliffe.com.

Thank you so much.
Tina Radcliffe

Questions for Discussion

1. The theme of this story is based on Philippians 3:13-14. "Brethren, I do not count myself to have apprehended; but one thing I do, forgetting those things which are behind and reaching forward to those things which are ahead, I press toward the goal for the prize of the upward call of God in Christ Jesus." Are you familiar with that verse? What does it mean to you?

2. We are to learn from our past but not live there. That also encompasses the area of forgiveness. Forgiving ourselves and others. Have you been in situations where you knew you had to forgive before you could move forward?

3. Dan and Beth both dealt with devastating abandonment crises that made them wary of trusting. Have you or has anyone you know had to face the same issue?

4. Beth's abandonment issues caused her to not realize her worth and be unable to see herself as others see her. Have you ever felt this way? What did you do to try to overcome these feelings?

5. Elsie is a very quirky character—a strong

woman who raised four children and buried a husband. She's very close to her children. Do you share a similar bond with your parents? How did that bond, or the absence of it, affect you growing up?

6. When Dan and Beth first meet he makes some assumptions about her as a city girl. Those assumptions are based on his own history. Have you ever found yourself making assumptions based on the hurts in your past? Have you had to rethink those assumptions later?

7. Beth lives her life carefully, controlling and planning her steps according to her goals and her five-year plan. She pays homage to control. Surrender to God is the only way she can finally find freedom. Can you relate to this? Have you had areas in your life that you reluctantly gave up, only to find freedom?

8. We revisit the town of Paradise in this book. In the winter, mountain towns can be cut off from the world during bad weather. Forced proximity brings out the core of people's personality very quickly. Beth and Dan fell in love over a week of close proximity. Does this seem realistic to you? Why?

9. Humor is a big part of the Dan's personality. He teaches Beth to temper her problems with a dose of humor and look at life less seriously. Often gentle humor can defuse tense situations. Is humor something you can relate to? How do you use humor to smooth over difficult situations?

10. Emily Robbs is the midwife who delivers the baby in this story. For women living in rural areas home deliveries are a normal scenario. Statistics show that home birth is as safe, or safer, than hospital birth for low-risk women. There are many advantages, including the increased bonding and lower stress for the mother. Have you known anyone who had a home delivery? Would you ever consider a home delivery for yourself or a member of your family?

11. Dan returned home like the prodigal son. He was able to admit his mistakes and ask his family for forgiveness. He was welcomed back with loving arms. Have you known someone who left home and returned, needing their family's loving arms? How did that situation work out?

12. Beth comes to know God by praying and finally asking Him into her heart. Are you familiar with the prayer she prayed? John 3:16 "For God

so loved the world, that He gave His only Son, that whoever believes in Him should not perish but have eternal life." What does that verse mean to you, personally?

13. In the church in New York City, Beth forgives her mother and accepts God's unconditional love. It can be very difficult to forgive someone who has wronged you but has no feelings of remorse. Have you ever experienced this?

14. Think about what an alternative ending might be for this book.

15. What do you think is the next step for Dan and Beth Gallagher?

LARGER-PRINT BOOKS!

GET 2 FREE
LARGER-PRINT NOVELS
PLUS 2 FREE
MYSTERY GIFTS

Love Inspired®

SUSPENSE
RIVETING INSPIRATIONAL ROMANCE

Larger-print novels are now available...